MATT HELM®
The War Years
A Pastiche

By Keith Wease
Based on the works of Donald Hamilton

Introduction

This book started on a whim several years ago. I was on vacation at a campsite beside a lake in South Texas, across from Louisiana, prepared to re-read the Matt Helm series for the umpteenth time. As I started *Death of a Citizen*, I began wondering just how much information Donald Hamilton had included about Matt's early days during the war. I made notes of any references to Matt's previous career, as well as biographical details. By the end of the vacation, I had finished the first dozen or so books and continued at home with the rest. As the series "aged," the war references stopped for obvious reasons, but I still got some more biographical information from the later books.

At the time, I was working in a one-man shop doing professional writing for clients and had a lot of "down" time. Going through my notes and the books, I transcribed all the references into my computer, including a few favorite passages typical of Donald Hamilton's amazing descriptive talent. I organized the file into an arbitrary timeline for my own amusement. Once this was done, I had a fairly accurate, if rather sketchy, portrayal of Matt Helm's early career and biography, enough for about a 25-page essay. Other than trivia for myself and other Matt Helm fans, it had no practical purpose whatsoever. I toyed with the idea of sending it to Donald Hamilton in the hopes he might be persuaded to give us a prequel, but gave up the idea as presumptuous. I saved the file to a disk and pretty much forgot about it.

Shortly after I learned that Donald Hamilton had died, I got the idea of writing the prequel myself. I located the disk and, as time and my imagination permitted, I filled in details for the various missions I already had, invented many more, and fleshed out my ideas of Matt's initial recruitment and training. My first complete chapters were the first and the last, once I had decided how to start and end the book. A couple of years later, I still needed two or three more chapters, including the one leading back to where the book began, but life got in the way for two or three more years before I finally finished it.

I spent the next year and a half trying to track down Donald Hamilton's heirs to get permission to publish the book, but all I could find were old references and old addresses. Finally, a random search brought up a post on some blog by the ex-husband of one of Donald Hamilton's daughters. I emailed him and he forwarded the email to his ex-wife. She responded directly to me and, once I explained the situation, sent an email to Gordon Hamilton, the CEO of *Integute AB*, the company he and his father had formed to hold his father's intellectual property rights. Gordon emailed me and graciously agreed to read my manuscript. After several back and forth emails over the next year, including some valuable editing advice, Gordon approved the book and we had a contract. Thanks, Gordon!

In closing, I'd like to make a point about my inclusion of verbatim quotes from Donald Hamilton's books. While being comfortable mimicking his "voice," I was not comfortable changing his words, so I chose not to rewrite those passages and included them as originally written by him.

Keith Wease, 2013

MATT HELM®
The War Years
A Pastiche

Chapter 1

Lying in the Army hospital near Washington, I had a lot of free time to reflect upon Mac's offer. Officially, I was recuperating from a near-fatal jeep accident and undergoing physical therapy to restore full mobility to various parts of my anatomy. Well, the physical therapy part was correct - my left arm and leg were just now beginning to work properly - but the jeep was largely imaginary, unless you counted being bounced around for three days in the back of a German Mercedes-Benz L4500A as an accident.

There were occasions during those three days when I'd wished they'd left me to die, rather than beat me to death slowly. Fortunately, I was unconscious most of the time, but my waking moments were filled with agony as we bounced and bumped along back roads - and quite often no roads - to avoid German patrols and make it back behind the front line to a field hospital. From there, I'd spent a lot of time in various hospitals before ending up here for some fairly specialized treatment.

The "accident" was no accident; the bastard had meant to kill me. Well, I'd tried to kill him first, so I couldn't really blame him and it was my own stupidity that had given him the chance in the first place. I'd naively assumed that half a magazine from the old MP38 I'd appropriated had killed him and hadn't made sure before turning to take out his partner. He had managed to pull the pin on the grenade and toss it in my general direction. Fortunately for me and unfortunately for his partner, the grenade had landed behind a tree, partially shielding me from the blast, but blowing his partner to hell and gone. I vaguely remember cursing myself as I was lifted and thrown like a leaf by the pile-driver blow that slammed into my left side....

The only thing I remember clearly from the following weeks, other than the pain, was looking up at Martinson as he helped load me into the back of some vehicle. I had a terrible feeling of something important left undone. Sensing the unspoken question in my eyes, he whispered, "It's okay, Eric, I made the touch." Satisfied that the job had gotten done despite my blunder, I lapsed back into unconsciousness.

I'd briefly seen Mac in the London hospital where most of the final repairs had been accomplished, some five weeks and four operations later. Apparently I was going to live and even get to keep my left leg - there had been some doubt for a while, due to a particularly nasty infection that could have gone either way. Mac had told me I was being transferred to Washington for some plastic surgery. We needed to cover up some potentially embarrassing round scars which were inconsistent with my cover as an Army Public Relations Officer who had never seen combat, but had been dumb enough to overturn a jeep near Paris.

I was now remembering our conversation earlier in the day. Mac had come into my room wearing a medium weight gray suit - even though it was spring over here, it was still a little cool outside. I had never seen him without a suit and never in any color but gray; just different weights, depending on the weather.

"Good morning, Eric. You seem to be recovering nicely." My real name, if it matters, is Matthew L. Helm, but in Mac's organization I was known as Eric, a name he'd apparently chosen due to my Scandinavian heritage. Except under special circumstances, we always used our code names when on official business. Of course, with Mac, everything was official business. I still knew nothing more about his background or personal life than the first time I met him, over three years before. Hell, I didn't even know his real name.

I sat up in the bed, a little painfully. "Yes sir, everything seems to be working right, finally." I thought I saw his lips twitch into a brief smile at the "sir" - it had been a small joke between us since our first meeting - but I could have been wrong; he wasn't really a smiling man.

"I understand the last of the more obvious scars have been covered."

"Yes sir, all seven of them. The Doc also took care of two stab wounds that seemed a little excessive for peaceful little me. That only leaves me with a half dozen or so, caused by pieces of my imaginary jeep landing on me. May I ask why you've gone to all this trouble? Not that I don't appreciate it - at least I think I do. I'm not sure which hurt more, the bullet or covering up the scar." I seemed to be sore all over. I wouldn't have believed how painful plastic surgery could be.

"Bullet wounds always raise a few eyebrows, especially for a known noncombatant. We like to be thorough when we construct a cover, as you know. Besides, you wouldn't want to shock your lady friend."

I gave him a sharp glance. How he'd found out about Beth I had no idea, but I shouldn't have been surprised. There was damn little that ever got past him. I decided not to ask. "What now, sir, the Pacific?" I already knew that our particular role in the war in Europe - actually, everybody's role, other than the mopping-up crew - was over.

"I think not, Eric. You did quite well in Europe." I was flattered; coming from Mac, this was high praise. He continued dryly, "However I can't quite envision a six foot four, two hundred pound, blond Swede with blue eyes infiltrating Tojo's army."

I grinned. "You may have a point, sir. But it's not two hundred pounds - not yet, but I'm gaining on it." I had lost over twenty pounds in the first three weeks and had only got back ten of it so far.

"In any case, the Pacific is not our kind of war. There's a new kind of war coming, Eric, one which will require our particular talents."

"You mean the Russians?" I had had similar thoughts. Even though they were still considered our allies, I had a feeling that wouldn't last long once Hitler was taken care of.

"Soviets, please." Mac was always precise in his language. "Yes, in the immediate future. However, the world is a savage place, and once a weapon has been developed, it tends to be used when needed. I foresee a use for our specialized type of weapon for a long time to come."

I should have known. Mac wasn't the type to just fade away and he had some very definite ideas when it came to solutions to problems of a violent nature. To the very few who were aware of our existence, we were known as the *M-Group*, "M" meaning "murder." Actually, the name had been suggested by the Germans. Their word was *Mordgruppe*, and the counter-intelligence people in Britain began picking up whispers of such an Allied organization from their spies in Germany. They thought it was just an excuse dreamed up by some German bureaucrats to explain certain failures - after all, we wouldn't stoop to such underhanded methods, would we? - but for those in the know, the name stuck.

I hadn't given much thought to what I would do once the war was over - at least not until very recently, after meeting Beth. She was a slim, lovely New England girl who was working at the hospital with the USO. I had met her a little over a month ago and we had hit it off big. So big, that I found myself thinking rather strange thoughts.

Mac brought me out of my reverie. "Eric, we are preparing your discharge papers. In the next few days, you'll be out of the Army and free to do whatever you want." Again, he surprised me. He seemed to know what I was thinking. He continued, and I knew what was coming.

"We will also be out of the military, if we were ever really in it. I have received permission to continue our little operation under civilian authority, never mind just *which* authority. If you'll consider it, I would like to have you continue with us. I have a

9

feeling this will be a bigger decision for you than it might have been a few weeks ago, so I'll give you time to think it over. The doctors tell me you'll be ready for release in another few days. Let me know your decision at that time."

I couldn't think of anything to say other than, "Yes sir." He turned and left. Well, he never was much for pleasantries or long goodbyes.

Check to the gent in the pajamas with the stupid look on his face, bandages covering half his body and a scary, half-formed idea of the future beginning to percolate in his thick skull.

Chapter 2

How he'd ever managed to sell the project to someone in authority, I never found out. It must have taken some doing, since America is a fairly sentimental and moral nation, even in wartime, and since all armies, including ours, have their book of rules, and this was certainly not in the books.

Exactly why he - or whomever he used for recruiting purposes - picked me, I never found out for certain. After all, I had the impression there were very few of us - an elite few I often thought in youthful enthusiasm - although I didn't know for sure. Curiosity wasn't encouraged and we operated on the principle that what we didn't know, we couldn't be forced to tell. I just didn't think there were that many people suited to that type of work, but why me in particular?

Certainly I fit the basic profile. I had been a hunter before the war. Mac liked to get men who'd done some hunting; it was the first thing he looked for in a prospective candidate. It wasn't that you couldn't train city boys to be just as efficient, as far as the mechanics of the job were concerned, he explained to me once, but they tended to lack the balance of men who were accustomed to going out once a year to shoot something specific, under definite legal restrictions. A city kid, turned loose with a gun, either took death too seriously and made a great moral issue of the whole business - and generally finished by cracking up under a load of self-imposed guilt - or, finding himself free of restraint for the first time in his life, turned into a crazed butcher. What criterion Mac used for the women - yes, we had some - I don't know.

Another reason Mac may have been interested in me was a different skill, one less common than marksmanship or hunting. As a kid I'd been interested in all kinds of weapons, but particularly in the edged ones. My parents were Scandinavian and I was a red-hot Viking aficionado as a kid. I read every gory old Norse saga I could get my hands on. I was crazy about the old battle-axe. I particularly liked H. Rider Haggard, who specialized in African adventure tales. His best-known book is probably *King Solomon's Mines*, but I read them all; and the one I remember best was called *Allan Quartermain*. Allan was the wise white hunter, and his native sidekick was the great Zulu warrior Umslopogaas, one of my favorite fictional characters at that youthful time. Umslopogaas carried an outsized battle-axe and died nobly, shattered axe in hand, holding a palace stairway against overwhelming odds. The inhabitants of Umslopogaas's home village were known as the People of the Axe. I guess it's the Viking in me. Guns are fine, but I'm an old sword-and-dagger man at heart. All through college, I'd been on the fencing team, and a few of us played around after classes with throwing knives. During Officers' training, I was one of the best with the bayonet. I enjoyed shooting, and my marksmanship scores were high in the expert range, but I looked forward with more anticipation to bayonet classes.

However, there are still an awful lot of people to choose from who are expert with both guns and knives of one sort or the other. Personally, I think Mac had a spy in the Army's Officer Training School, one of the instructors, who recommended me.

Like many young men of my age, I joined the Army a few months after Pearl Harbor. For me, it was a matter of conscience. Although born here, I was first generation. My parents had immigrated from Sweden, changing their name in the process. It was originally Stjernhjelm, but my father shortened it to Helm, chopping it down to something Yankees could pronounce when he got to America. From the time I was born - well, actually I'm not sure of that, but at least from the time I could understand speech - my parents spoke English around the house. Maybe they spoke Swedish in the privacy of their bedroom, but all I heard was English until I was old enough that it was my primary language, then they taught me some Swedish. They had very firm ideas of loyalty. We were now Americans, this was our country and we would speak and act as everybody else did. Of course they never entirely got rid of the accent, but they made damned sure it didn't rub off on me. I think my dad was a bigger patriot than most of those born in America, an attitude he shared with a large percentage of immigrants, and it must have been passed on to me. Call it loyalty, call it patriotism, but my country was at war and my duty was clear.

Thanks to a degree in journalism, acquired shortly before my parents died, I was considered officer material and sent to OTS. Although I was a journalist of sorts, having got a job with a camera on a newspaper in Santa Fe, New Mexico after graduation, and then working for some other New Mexico newspapers, the last being in Albuquerque, I requested infantry training rather than accepting a position in Public Relations. My drill instructor, a grizzled veteran named March - as in the month - approved and seemed to take a liking to me.

One day, I got into a fight. Well, it wasn't much of a fight as fights go. I'd never been sold on fists as a way to settle anything. First of all, you can't do much damage that way - at least I can't - and second, you often leave someone very mad at you, someone you haven't damaged enough to stop from getting revenge. There's a third reason; when you hit someone in the mouth with your fist, damn it, it hurts!

Although the instructors tried to keep it to a minimum, there were always fights getting started. After all, we were at war. We were going to go kill us some Nazis and the adrenaline was flowing. Put that together with a bunch of young, eager new recruits and something has to explode occasionally. Mine started the way they usually do. His name, as I remember, was Cameron. He was a hell of a big man, not quite my height - very few are - but much wider and heavier with the craggy face of the professional muscleman. His nose had been broken many years ago. It could have happened in college football, but somehow I didn't think so. You know the type. There's something tight about the mouth and eyes, something contemptuous and condescending, and he didn't like me a bit. I don't know if it was jealousy - I had beaten him badly in both bayonet and judo classes - or if he just disapproved of my loner attitude. I don't make friends easily and have never been much for team sports. I'd refused his offer to join the baseball team they'd organized when off-duty.

Whatever it was, he'd decided to take me down a peg right after rifle practice. He said something nasty by way of preamble. I ignored him and turned away and he made the mistake of grabbing my arm and spinning me around. As I turned, I saw his fist cocked to hit me. I was amazed. After all, I was still holding my rifle; grabbing and threatening someone holding a firearm doesn't come under the heading of the brightest - or safest - idea in the world. Of course, he was one of the muscle boys, the type who always thinks first of using his hands. It never occurs to them that someone else might think otherwise. I briefly considered shooting him, but the rifle was a little out of position and he was too close. I won't pretend that the idea that the Army would take a dim view of one recruit shooting another didn't play a part in my decision, but it wasn't an overriding concern. Besides, I didn't need to shoot him to win. I simply brought up the rifle and broke his jaw with the butt.

With an innocent look on my face, I bent over him and said loudly, "Hey man, I'm sorry. Are you all right?" It was wasted on him; he was out cold. I got a couple of fellow recruits to help me carry him to the infirmary. When I came out, my instructor, March, pulled me off to the canteen for a beer.

Once we were seated with our beers - I don't really like the stuff, but hard liquor was prohibited during training - March asked me, "Why didn't you shoot?"

I looked at him contemplatively for a moment before discarding the idea of playing innocent. He knew better. I simply replied, "It wasn't necessary."

"You thought about it, though. I could tell. I saw the look in your eyes and thought he was dead. You stopped the impulse in time, which showed good sense, but why hit him with the butt? Why not just fight it out like the others do?"

"I don't fight for fun and he's too big to take with my bare hands. That judo stuff we've been practicing is fine when both people observe the rules, but I don't think he'd play fair. He'd just beat the hell out of me." I let out a pent-up breath. The anger was beginning to subside, the anger I always feel when I come up against the attitude that Cameron represented. I don't know why, but I felt I had to explain myself to this old warrior.

"Look, I'm tired of people who think they are so tough that they can do whatever they want and the rest of us should just lay down and take it. I won't take it and I refuse to play by the rules. All anybody's ever had to do to stay perfectly safe and healthy in my neighborhood is to leave me alone. If someone chooses not to and opens the gate, I figure I am at liberty to walk as far in as I choose."

"How old are you, Helm - 22, maybe 23?" I nodded. "How does someone that young develop that attitude?" He wasn't criticizing, I saw. He was actually curious, in an approving sort of way. Well, he'd been around the block and survived. Maybe he'd understand.

"I got that way in college, the first college I went to, a real gung-ho place. It had a kind of ornamental pool, called the Lily Pond, although it was mostly muck and weeds. The upper classmen, if they disapproved of the behavior of a lower classman, had the cute habit of descending on him in force, dragging him out to this glorified mud puddle, and heaving him in. It was kind of an old school tradition.

"Well, one day the grapevine let me know I was next on the dunking list. I'd been expecting it. I'd been planning on upholding the school honor in such individual sports as fencing and rifle-shooting, but the seniors had decided I ought to go out for basketball because of my height. I'd told them frankly that if there was anything that turned my stomach, it was team sports of any kind, particularly the ones that became college religions. That hadn't gone over real big, if you know what I mean. Well, I just didn't feel like an involuntary bath that evening, so I laid out a hunting knife and wedged a chair under the doorknob of my room.

15

It was a fairly feeble old chair and the back was cracked, but nobody knew that but me. I just wanted some evidence that they'd actually broken in. There weren't any locks in that dormitory that worked. It was a real togetherness institution. You weren't supposed to want privacy, ever. That was considered antisocial and un-American.

"Well, they came. There was the usual loudmouthed, beery mob. They yelled at me to open the door. I called back that I hadn't invited them, and if they wanted in, they knew what to do. They did it. The first one inside after they'd smashed the door open was the big school-spirit expert who'd given me the pep talk about how I didn't want to let the college and the basketball team down. He was very brave. He told me not to be silly, I wasn't really going to use that knife, just put it down. I told him if he put a hand on me, I'd cut it off. So he did; and I did. Well, not all the way off. I understand they sewed it back together and he got some use out of it eventually. Nevertheless, the immediate result was a lot of groans and gore, very spectacular. I told the rest it was a sample, and I had plenty more if anybody wanted it. Nobody did."

"Wasn't that just a tad drastic?" March asked.

"I know, they were boys who were obviously just tight and having a little fun. And they could have gone and had their tight little fun anywhere they damned well pleased, except in my room at my expense. I made that quite clear to them before the action started. They chose to ignore the warning. That made it open hunting season by my way of reckoning. I figured - then and now - that anybody who invaded my domicile by force is mine if I can take him. Anybody who lays hands on me without my permission is fair and legal game. Anybody who opens the door to violence has simply got no legitimate beef if a little more violence walks in than he bargained for. As far as I'm concerned, people can either stick to polite, civilized conduct, or I'll give them jungle all the way."

"What happened after that - legally, I mean?"

"Hell, the school authorities couldn't do anything to *me*. I was the aggrieved party, wasn't I, the victim of unprovoked aggression? I mean, there I was in my room, studying hard and minding my own business like a good little freshman. A bunch of hoodlums breaks in and, outnumbered though I am, I defended myself bravely. Wouldn't you think I'd be in line for a hero medal, or something? They said I didn't have to use a *knife*, and I said of course I had to use a knife. Or a gun. What was I supposed to do, beat up a dozen older boys, including some outsized football types, with my bare fists? Superman, I'm not. To stop them, without actually killing anybody, I had to do something swift and bloody and dramatic to show I meant business right at the start. I did just about the least drastic thing that could get my point across. They threw me out of that school, of course. Having a weapon in my room was the official excuse. The broken chair, proving they'd forced their way in, saved me from being sued or arrested for assault, but nobody ever did anything about any of the others besides a sort of token reprimand. And at that point, I realized I was just a little out of step with the rest of the world, a world where you're supposed to let people heave you into fishponds any time they happen to feel like it. I decided I'd better look around, once I'd finished getting my degree elsewhere, and see if I couldn't find at least a few characters marching to my kind of music. I still haven't found them yet. I kind of hoped to find them here, but it's the same old thing."

I stopped to take a breath, waiting for his reaction. I still often find the old anger coming back that always hits me when I meet that kind of guy; the kind that broke into my room that night, the kind that's always pushing people around and always gets terribly, terribly shocked and self-righteous when he runs into somebody who's willing to die, or kill, rather than put up with his overbearing nonsense.

March watched me quietly, waiting for the punch line, not saying anything. After a moment, I continued.

"There was a kind of epilogue. Three years after the incident I read in the papers that there was a big scandal at that school.

17

Another bunch of arrogant seniors had got hold of another poor dumb freshman whose behavior wasn't to their liking; and they'd given him the old school heave - only, it turned out, there was some kind of a rusty drainpipe out there in the muck that nobody'd ever noticed. He landed right on it. The last I heard, he was still alive, if you can call it living. He can blink his eyelids once for yes and twice for no, or vice versa. And every time I think of him, I remember my old hunting knife with much affection. If it hadn't been for those six inches of cold, sharp steel, that human vegetable might have been me."

We sat there a while, drinking our beers and not saying anything. I got the impression that my instructor knew exactly the way I felt and was simply waiting for my adrenalin rush to subside. He was the first person I had ever told that story - why, I couldn't really say. Maybe it was just the look of him, a predator with the smell of gunpowder about him, and why that thought came into my mind is anybody's guess.

He gave me a wolfish grin. "You're all right, Helm. You realize you don't really fit in here, don't you?"

"I know," I grinned back. "Can't you just see me as the gung-ho leader, getting his troops all pumped up for God and country? Hell, with my attitude, one of them would probably shoot me in the back as we went up the hill. Maybe I shouldn't have accepted a commission."

"Have you considered sniper school? Your scores are certainly good enough, and you've got the right instincts."

I frowned. "Not really. I didn't know they selected officers for sniper duty."

"Normally they don't. But I've heard of a new program being considered, sort of a commando outfit. They don't seem too particular whether it's bars or stripes that determine your rank. They're more concerned with results. If you're interested, I'll ask around."

18

"I'm interested."

"Good enough. By the way, don't worry about that little fracas. You set it up with that innocent act. I'll make sure it sticks."

"Thanks, Sarge." I'd found it interesting that most of the field instructors were enlisted, while the classroom instructors were officers. It seemed kind of backwards to me. Shouldn't the leaders be the best fighters? Welcome to the modern military. As he'd said, I didn't really fit in, but what the hell - you do your duty. Nobody ever promised you'd enjoy it.

Two weeks later, after pinning the shiny new gold bar on my lapel, I was offered a chance for some special training; objective vague, unit unspecified, mission classified. I grabbed it. Like I said - a spy.

Chapter 3

I was shipped off to a place in Arizona, called the Ranch, never mind exactly where. We went through some pretty silly procedures involving several detours and an open door on a parked vehicle before we pulled up in front of a shiny new gate at the end of an old weather-beaten dirt road. As the driver got out to open the gate, I had the feeling of being watched. Nobody else was in sight, but I didn't think I would want to open that gate without the appropriate authorization. It was that kind of a place.

It had been a long drive and I was tired and bored and it was late. The driver had introduced himself as Frank and that was practically the last word he said, other than polite inquiries concerning food and sanitary needs. We drove past a couple of low buildings with a few people milling around. No one paid us any attention, which was strange. You'd think simple curiosity, if nothing else, would warrant a stare or two.

A short distance away, we stopped in front of a small bungalow. Frank told me to take my things inside and wait until someone came to brief me. I was not to wander around, but to stay inside. It was the longest sentence I'd heard from him. Then he surprised me. As I started toward the front door, he waved and said, "Good luck." It made him seem almost human. Almost.

They didn't make me wait long. I'd just managed to unpack a little and splash some water on my face - the bungalow was a miniature hotel room with its own bathroom complete with shower, which was okay with me since I don't fit too well in the average bathtub - when a well-built, medium-sized guy walked in without knocking. He was quite a handsome and distinguished-looking man with thick, black well-combed hair. He also had a look much like March, my drill instructor. I don't mean that they looked anything alike. It was the bearing, a hint of danger and, as I'd said before, the smell of gunpowder that is perceived by the brain if not by the

20

nose. I think that was the first time I started getting the feeling I'd found a home.

He smiled and held out his hand. "The name's Vance, and you're Helm." It wasn't a question.

I shook his hand, noticing that he felt no need to assert his masculinity with a knuckle-grinding clutch, as I would have expected from my first impression. It was just a nice, firm handshake. "Are you the guy who's going to explain what I'm doing here?" I asked.

"To a certain extent. I'm going to be your trainer for a while. Are you hungry?"

"Starving."

"Let's go over to the canteen and grab a bite and I'll explain as much as I can."

He led me to one of the low buildings I'd noticed, entering through a door on one end, the East end if it matters. He went first and I noticed a bulge under his coat, up against his spine about belt level. I wondered if it was what I thought it was. As we entered, it was apparent that half the building had been divided into a combination cafeteria and bar. Only a couple tables were occupied. We went through the serving line, both of us helping ourselves to something that vaguely resembled roast beef and some watery mashed potatoes. At least we had a choice of vegetables. I picked peas while Vance went for the corn. A couple soggy rolls topped off our plates. There seemed to be plenty of food, if a limited choice; however, there were no people in sight behind the counter. A door led off the back to what I assumed was a kitchen.

Vance headed toward a back table, well away from the other diners, and I followed, careful not to stumble on the rough wood floor. The whole place looked like a hastily-converted bunkhouse with no attention being given to dressing it up. I kept wondering what happened to the horses. I mean, it was obviously some kind

21

of horse ranch. Having been brought up in New Mexico, I grew up around the corrals where the interesting characters hung out. I felt right at home.

In between bites, Vance told me what I could expect during my time here. "You're on a sort of probation," he said. "You've got some specialized abilities we're interested in and an aptitude for acquiring some others. That's *my* job. There are a few other things to be determined before we decide to keep you around, but you'll find out what those are as we go."

I started to object and then decided against it.

Vance smiled. "That's one, self control. I don't like blowhards, no matter how good they are - or think they are. We're going to get along just fine."

I rather doubted that. There was just a little tension between us and I wasn't sure why. I figured it out later, of course. This kind of business tends to attract loners and, as a rule we - I'm definitely included in that category - don't get along "just fine." Most of the time we're wondering if we can take the other by hand or if we'll need a gun...

He continued, "We have a rather unique training program. There's one instructor to each student, at least in the beginning. This is a highly classified operation and if you don't make the grade, you can be returned to your former branch of the service - in your case the Army - without too much interesting information in your head.

"Here's the way it goes. For the next few weeks, I'm your chaperone. You don't eat, walk, shit or even look at another person without me around. You do get to sleep by yourself, and any free time is spent in your room, not that you'll have much free time. In between learning new skills, we'll concentrate on refining existing ones. Any questions?"

"No, sir." I mean, he'd made it quite clear. I was in the Army; I was used to taking orders, even stupid, meaningless and totally nonsensical orders. They're all security happy in the military and if it made them feel good to say "Top Secret" every time they didn't want to tell you something, who was I to complain? But I made up my mind that I would take everything this guy told me with a grain of salt.

He bent forward a bit and reached behind him. I tensed a little as he brought out the standard Army-issue Colt .45 automatic, Model 1911, black and deadly-looking. He laid it on the table and pushed it toward me, watching carefully.

The hell with him. I hadn't needed the Army course to respect firearms. I grew up with them, including one just like this that my father had owned. I picked it up and, turning in my chair to point it downward, popped out the magazine to make sure it was loaded and checked the chamber to see if there was a cartridge in it. There wasn't. Well, you don't carry a pistol in your belt with a cartridge chambered, not if you want to keep all the various parts of your anatomy in working order. I slipped the magazine back in and made sure the safety was set.

"Very good," he said as I grinned at him. "That's yours for the duration. Your job is to learn it to the point you can strip and reassemble it blindfolded, and that's not a figure of speech. Then we'll teach you how to shoot it."

"I know how to shoot it. My dad had one."

"You just think you know. Just like you think you know a lot of things." He held up his hand to stop me, but I was disciplined. I wasn't going to protest. I was just going to wait and show him. He nodded in approval and went on, smiling.

"I'm not being obnoxious. I'm just being honest. I had a lot of training before I came here the first time and thought I knew everything there was to know about shooting, too. We all do, until we go through this very specialized course."

I smiled back, relaxing a little. Maybe he wasn't such a jackass after all. "Okay, you're the boss. When do we get started?"

"First thing in the morning. Get a good night's sleep, 'cause you'll need it. I'll be by at six o'clock to take you to breakfast."

Chapter 4

They've got a funny damn way of waking you up in that place. First they tell you what time to get up so you can set your alarm clock. Then, about an hour or so before that, they walk into your room and start shooting holes in the ceiling with a cannon. Well, it's not really a cannon, just a little old .45, and he didn't really shoot holes in the ceiling. He used blanks. At least I hoped they were blanks - in that place you never knew for sure.

That first morning, Vance walked into my room at about four o'clock and fired off three shots. I came out of the bed like a shot - pun intended - and crashed to the floor all wrapped up in the bedclothes. Even then, to my later satisfaction, I had enough presence of mind to crawl under the bed with my shorts unsoiled. That, of course, wasn't the proper response, but at least I was thinking and not just scared shitless. The scatological terminology is Vance's. He told me later that a lot of the recruits actually shit themselves - which I guess, is how the phrase originated.

When I heard Vance laughing, I crawled out from under the bed as he turned on the light. I didn't hit him - after all I knew he had a gun - I just thought about it. He could tell what I was thinking and, to my amazement, grinned in approval.

"Good," he said, "you don't scare easily. That's the biggest step."

I was beginning to realize that this had been part of my training, not just a stupid prank. "The hell I wasn't scared," I yelled. "I damn near had a heart attack."

"That's permissible, just as long as you're not too scared to act. Some of the kids we get here are on their way back out the first time I pull this trick on them." He was a fine one to talk about kids - he couldn't be more than a year or two older than me - but in dangerous professions, especially the military, the "kid" label is applied more by experience, or lack thereof, than by chronology.

"Where's your gun?" When I nodded toward the beat-up dresser against the wall, he walked over and picked it up and tossed it to me. I think that scared me more than the shots he'd fired. I'd been taught never to throw a loaded gun - they have a nasty habit of going off when dropped, something you never see in the movies where they're forever pitching pistols around with no loud bangs.

I caught the .45 with both hands open, cushioning it. You don't grab at it; you might grab the trigger. I quickly checked the pistol since it had been out of my possession for a while. I saw a note of respect in Vance's eyes. It seemed to be my day for compliments, spoken and unspoken.

"I see you don't go in for loaded guns flying through the air. Neither do I. Just so you don't get the wrong idea, it's not loaded - well not really. Those are blanks." I removed the magazine and looked at it. The bullets looked real to me, not the flat wads that are usually stuffed into the shell in blank cartridges. "Oh, those are real bullets, there's just no powder in the cartridges," he explained as he saw my puzzled expression. "We can't afford to lose any instructors to overanxious or scared recruits."

He walked over and handed me a new magazine. "Here are some real ones for later. Leave the one with blanks on the dresser so you can put it back in tonight. Get dressed and let's go to breakfast."

Apparently, the canteen never closed. This time, the counter was filled with scrambled eggs, hash browns, bacon and that uniquely military concoction, politely called "SOS" -shit on a shingle for you more vulgar types. Actually, I kind of liked it, although - like every other G.I. - I'd never admit it out loud. Vance preferred the eggs, at least this morning.

This time, we were the only ones in the place. I decided that the cook must sneak in and out when nobody's around, being the shy sort. Vance seemed to be uncomfortable just eating and continued to talk as we ate. "Rule one, always keep your gun handy, even in bed. Don't put it under the pillow; that's the first place someone will look. Put it down under the covers, alongside your thigh. After a couple nights you get used to it and stop rolling over on top of it or knocking it on the floor."

"Who do you expect to come looking for it - besides you, I mean?"

He laughed. "Just anyone in general. You'll be going into combat eventually, of a sort. Just pay attention. Okay if I call you Matt?"

"Sure, why not?"

"Okay, Matt. This morning was important and it will continue for a while. The idea is to teach you to wake up ready. The next time you're rudely woken up - awakened? - I want to see you come up with the gun in your hand. We'll continue practicing until it's second nature to you. Until then, keep the blanks in the gun at night. We don't want to lose me, okay?"

"Gotcha. Grab gun full of blanks."

"Or a knife. Or any other weapon you can get your hands on. Most people waking up someone from a sound sleep expect him to be groggy and disoriented. If you wake up ready, with a gun in your hand, you may buy those extra seconds that is the difference between you dead and the other guy dead."

I nodded, more serious this time. I was beginning to get the idea - and liking it.

After breakfast, we went back to my bungalow and Vance had me practice field stripping the .45 until it got light outside. We then got into the jeep he'd brought with him earlier that morning, and drove out to the practice range - one of them. There seemed to be several. Well, it's a pretty desolate country out there in the southwest and there are lots of wide open spaces. The pistol range had the usual man-sized silhouette targets and Vance had me fire off several dozen practice rounds - with each hand - to get the feel of the .45. I discovered later that practicing with the weak hand was a matter of official policy, not just Vance's idea.

27

After deciding I was a pretty good shot, at least with my right hand, we got down to serious business. Vance went to the jeep and pulled out a bag of round, white plastic Ping-Pong balls, each a little smaller than a golf ball. He walked downrange about thirty-five feet and dropped several on the ground. Returning, he told me, "See if you can hit one of these. No, don't aim, just point and shoot."

I got one. It only took me seven shots. The second one only took me five shots. Vance came over and took the gun from me and slipped in a new magazine. Turning quickly, he pulled the trigger four times and four white balls jumped up into the air. He reached into the bag with his left hand and took out two more balls. Throwing them into the air downrange, he hit both before they started back down. I was impressed and said so.

"It's called trick shooting," he explained. "It is accomplished by just yanking out your gun and firing, not seeing the sights, not seeing the gun, even; not seeing anything but the mark. Wishing the bullet home; and if you do it right, with enough concentration, you can toss a marble into the air and hit it with the pellet from a BB gun held at the hip. It seems like magic. Just how it works, nobody's ever told me, but it works, if you *think* the slug home. That is, it works if you're in practice. You have to practice, to keep the concentration."

He paused, letting it sink in. "Try it again. Forget the gun, just concentrate on the ball." I did, getting four out of ten. I kept trying, getting better and better. He was right; the more I concentrated, the more shots went where I wanted them to go. I was enjoying myself and he couldn't get me away from the range until we ran out of balls. Within two weeks, I could even shoot one of them out of the air, but I never did get good enough to match his two.

In the ensuing days, I practiced with a variety of pistols and found one that fit me perfectly. It was a beautiful - to me - .22 Colt Woodsman and I fell in love. Vance noticed my preference and told me I could keep it if I liked those little toys. I made a few choice remarks about his noisy beast of a .45 and we ended up agreeing to disagree, in a friendly fashion. From pistols we went on to rifles - all kinds of rifles - where I did much better. Not as good as Vance at first, but close enough. He still managed to teach me a few things, and toward the end of my training we were pretty evenly matched.

I even got a chance to teach *him* something about rifles. He came up with a brand new .30-06 and had me sight it in. I got the telescopic sight roughly centered, so the shots would at least go on the paper at a hundred yards. A standard .30-06 is a lot of gun to shoot from rest, prone, where the body can't rock back with the recoil but has to stay and take the punishment. I started shooting for group, five rounds, using a different bullet weight for each target. You never know what bullet a gun is going to like best until you try it. After I'd finished, I went down to inspect the targets. I put a pocket ruler across the best group, the 150-grain load. Four and a quarter inches. A bolt-action rifle that won't group within two inches at a hundred yards isn't worth having, and I ought to get one and a half even with factory ammunition.

After putting up fresh targets, I got out the tools and took the gun apart. It looked like the stock had warped a little, which they often do on those light rifles. Vance looked at me in amazement.

"This isn't something they teach in training, is it?" I asked. I pointed at the stock. "It's supposed to be a free-floating barrel without any wood contact, but we seem to be getting some pressure here that's throwing it off. If I ream out the barrel channel a bit I can put in a few cardboard shims to free things up around the action." I finished as he watched in interest.

"Where did you learn that?" he finally asked.

"I picked it up as a kid. I always used to be crazy about guns. And knives and swords and all the rest of the stuff that tickles a kid's bloodthirsty imagination. That's probably why they picked me out of the Army after a couple months and put me into this outfit."

29

I slipped the bolt back into the rifle and shot another five with the 150-grain load. Satisfied, I sighted it in three inches high at a hundred yards. That'd put her just about on the button at two-fifty.

I could tell he was impressed. Regardless of any small friction between us, we were developing a healthy respect for one another.

By the end of the fourth week Vance was satisfied with my "wake-up-ready" responses - he'd vary the time and occasionally skip a night or two - and let me sleep uninterrupted. Not that he actually said anything - he just stopped waking me up and after a few days I assumed he was satisfied. This was a welcome relief because I needed all the sleep I could get at that point - we were into hand-to-hand combat and I was sore all the time.

It turned out Vance's specialty - aside from pistols - was a particularly lethal sport called *Okinawan Karate*, as distinguished from the more stylized and less deadly Japanese variety. It was several centuries old and not well-known in the U.S. He told me an immigrant *sensei* - teacher - from Okinawa had established a Karate school, called a *dojo*, in his home town and he'd spent several years learning the sport, eventually earning a Black Belt. It was an interesting combination of offense, defense and concentration - which probably explained his success at trick shooting.

Vance had added a few variations which, he said, would have dismayed his *sensei*, an essentially peaceful man. Apparently, the original form of Karate, while deadly to various boards and bricks, was less damaging to human beings - you were supposed to "pull" the blow and not actually touch your opponent, in training at least. The version Vance taught was based on the theory, "no pain, no gain." Oh, he pulled his punches, just enough not to really break anything while still getting the point across. For a while I had quite an assortment of bruises, but I learned, in self-defense. I learned over a half-dozen ways to kill a man with my bare hands and at least twenty bones that could be broken with just the edge of my hand.

30

I think to really get into the hand-to-hand stuff, you've got to start as a kid. I'd always been big enough to avoid most of the fights kids get into - not that I had that many opportunities, being brought up on a ranch outside town - and my father discouraged fist-fighting in any case. I really didn't think I could do much damage to anyone with any training, but I could handle any 90-pound weakling who wasn't looking. Apparently, Vance felt the same way. The last thing he said, disgusted, at the end of that phase of training was, "For Christ's sake, Matt, the idea is to disable or kill your opponent, not just get him pissed off. We'd better teach you to use a knife."

And that's what we did next, fortunately for my ego. Even from the start, Vance was no match for me with a knife - any kind of knife, even the long ones. Toward the end we had reversed roles and I was teaching him the finer points of fencing. Although I tried to conceal it, he could tell I was pleased with myself. What he said at that point stayed with me. "Matt," he said, "Don't worry about hurting my feelings. I learned a long time ago, when you come across a real expert who wants to help you, don't be proud, let him. Or her. En Garde."

I still think that the most important things Vance taught me had to do with attitude, not skill. Well, maybe that was the idea. We might never really be friends, but if he ever wants to tell me anything, I'll listen.

Shortly after that, Vance told me we were done with the first phase of my training and I was being sent to Washington D.C. for psychological testing and he hoped to see me back in a week or so for the final phase. Frank's brother picked me up - I suppose he really wasn't the brother of the driver who brought me to the Ranch, but he was as sparse with words and emotion as Frank - and drove me to the nearest airport, never mind the exact location. The next day I was starting the battery of tests designed to find out if I was really outrageously insane enough to join the outfit or just moderately crazy and only fitted for the Army. At least that was my impression. It didn't have to be right.

31

Chapter 5

Even after the training and the tests, I'll admit that I found the idea a little startling, even in wartime, when Mac first explained to me exactly what this group was that I'd been picked to join. I could still remember, very distinctly, the pep talk we'd got from Mac, each one of us new recruits, the first time we actually saw him. At least I suppose the others all got it, too, but I can't really speak for anyone but myself.

I remember the shabby little office - like all the subsequent shabby little offices in which I was to make my reports and receive my orders - and the compact, gray-haired man with the cold gray eyes, and the speech he gave while I stood before him at attention. The man was, I judged, a well-preserved forty-five, with the rangy, powerful build of a college football star who'd put on a little middle-aged weight and would have put on more if it hadn't been for the rowing machine and the handball court. His face had a hint of Lincolnesque angularity, of which he was aware. It was the only angularity about him. In all other respects he was a real smoothie. He was in civvies, and he hadn't called for any military courtesies. I didn't know his rank if he had any, but I wasn't taking any chances.

Somehow, I already knew this outfit was for me if they'd have me; and I wasn't too proud to take what advantage I could get from a good stiff back and liberal use of the word "sir." I'd already been in the Army long enough to know they'd practically give the joint to anybody who could shoot, salute and say "sir." Anyway, when you're six feet four, even if kind of skinny and bony, the word doesn't sound humble, merely nice and respectful.

"Yes, sir," I said, "I wouldn't mind learning why I've been assigned here, sir, if it's time for me to know."

He said, "You've got a good record, Helm. Handy with weapons. Westerner, aren't you?"

"Yes, sir."

"Hunter?"

"Yes, sir."

"Upland game?"

"Yes, sir."

"Waterfowl?"

"Yes, sir."

"Big game?"

"Yes, sir."

"Deer?"

"Yes, sir."

"Elk?"

"Yes, sir."

"Bear?"

"Yes, sir."

"Dress them out yourself?"

"Yes, sir. When I can't get somebody to help me."

"That's fine," he said. "For this job we need a man who isn't scared of getting his hands bloody."

He was looking at me in a measuring and weighing manner as he went into his talk. As he explained it, it was merely a matter of degree. I was in the Army anyway. If the enemy attacked my unit, I'd shoot back, wouldn't I? And when the orders came through for us to attack, I'd jump up and do my damnedest to kill some more. I'd be dealing with them *en masse* under these conditions; but I was known to be pretty good with a rifle, so in spite of my commission it wasn't beyond the realm of possibility that one day I'd find myself squinting through a telescopic sight, waiting for some individual poor dope to expose himself four or five hundred yards away. But I'd still just be selecting my victims by blind chance. What if I were offered the opportunity to serve my country in a less haphazard way?

Mac paused here, long enough to indicate that I was supposed to say something. I said, "You mean, go over and stalk them in their native habitat, sir?"

Chapter 6

My second trip to the ranch was more relaxed. Good old Frank was waiting at the airport to pick us up - I'd acquired a companion on the trip down from Washington, a guy called Daryl. That was his code name, as mine was Eric. After I'd failed to walk out in horror following my first meeting with Mac, I'd been assigned the name and instructed to use it exclusively on official business, including training. It wasn't really so much a cloak and dagger tactic as it was a means of giving each of us something to call the other without giving away unnecessary information such as our real names and ranks.

Daryl was older, in his late twenties, and, unlike me, had already had some combat experience before being recruited by Mac and was just a little smug about it - an attitude I was looking forward to erasing with a demonstration of my superior skills. I guess I qualified as being a little big-headed back then, too. Of course, both of us would have it knocked out of us very shortly. Daryl was my opposite in looks: just under five foot ten and stocky where I was tall and thin. He had short, dark-brown hair and brown eyes and the general look we usually defined as black Irish, although he had no trace of an Irish accent.

I disliked him on sight, probably because I've always had an instinctive distrust of brown eyes, a prejudice which I'll cheerfully admit is perfectly ridiculous. Daryl, on the other hand, seemed to take a liking to me in a condescending manner, and as training progressed, he kind of adopted me as his younger brother, more than once pulling someone off me when tempers flared. I gradually warmed up to him and, a few months later, felt ashamed of my initial feelings when he took a bullet pushing me out of the line of fire on our first mission. He came through it all right, but I felt like a heel.

Frank had greeted us like old comrades, surprising the hell out of me. It seemed I was past the probation period and was now part of the group, officially acknowledged and accepted rather than being treated like some intruder. It turned out that Frank was our surveillance and interrogation instructor and had come to us from Army Intelligence. He was friendly and talkative during our drive out to the Ranch, but I noticed he was careful not to give us any hint as to his personal life or background other than the reference to his former unit.

We went through the same routine as on my first visit, but this time people looked at us and actually waved as we drove up. Frank explained that the Ranch had been reserved for new recruits only the first time - Daryl had been there too, even though I'd never seen him. This time only the survivors were present for final training and security had been relaxed accordingly.

Frank let us off at a different bungalow this time and told us we were bunkmates. "You two are the last to arrive," he said. "Initial briefing is at twenty hundred in the opposite end of the canteen building. You've got about an hour to settle in and get a bite to eat. Don't be late."

I never did find out how many of us started the first phase of training, but only nine of us survived it - at least in this group. I found out later that we were the second such group. How the initial instructors were selected and trained I don't know and was afraid to ask. When Daryl and I walked into the canteen, everyone was there, including one woman, much to the surprise of both of us. Somehow I'd gotten the impression that this was a men-only club, which just goes to show you how wrong my first impressions often were.

I caught a glimpse of someone in an apron heading through the door behind the counter - our shy cook, I guessed - but otherwise it was laid out the same, even to the watery mashed potatoes and synthetic beef. I was mildly surprised to find the peas replaced by green beans. Apparently Mac - or whoever planned the menus - didn't feel we were entitled to anything spectacular by way of our culinary preferences, regardless of our highly regarded talents. Well, that was okay with me. As an old ranch hand, I'm a meat and potatoes man most of the time although I do like a freshly prepared fish now and then - preferably one I've caught myself.

As we found a table, there were nods of welcome and even a couple smiles, but nobody jumped up to introduce himself - or herself. Actually the woman was not bad looking, in a cold, calculating sort of way. Her red hair was trimmed a little shorter than I liked and her clear, green eyes looked considerably older and more experienced than the rest of her. There were no freckles that I normally associated with that color of hair and her mouth looked a little odd before I realized she had a hairline scar running from her left ear to the corner of her mouth. The rest of her was slim and taut in a pair of tight denims and some kind of a woolen blouse or shirt. Finishing it off was a worn pair of sneakers.

After that brief look due to the surprise of seeing a woman - girl, really; she couldn't be any older than my 23 - in that presumably male group, I turned away with no further masculine interest. I mean, as a good New Mexican, I lived in the land of blue jeans and squaw dresses, of bare brown legs and thong sandals, but I prefer the impractical, fragile, feminine look of a woman in a dress or skirt and stockings and high heels; and I can see no particular reason for a female to appear publicly in pants unless she's going to ride a horse. I'll even go so far as to say that the side-saddle and riding skirt made an attractive combination, and I regret that they passed before my time.

Please don't think this means I'm prudish and consider it sinful for women to reveal themselves in trousers. Quite the contrary. I object on the grounds that it makes my life very dull. We all respond to different stimuli, and the fact is that I don't respond at all to pants, no matter whom they may contain or how tight they may be. Daryl obviously didn't have my hang-ups and continued to stare at her until she glared back challengingly. With a faint flush of embarrassment, he also turned away and sat down next to me. "Looks like this might be more fun than I thought," he said in a low voice. "I wouldn't mind having a piece of that."

I looked over at him. "Yeah," I said. "Not bad at all."

I mean, with a certain type of guy, especially in the military or other organizations where men gather in groups, you've got to pretend to be leching after every woman in sight or he'll think you're not normal. It turned out that my new bunkmate was one of those who, having once started, could discuss the subject indefinitely while we ate and drank a couple of beers. I'd had a long day and I found it hard to keep from yawning. Not that sex itself bores me you understand, but talking about it just seems like a pointless form of masturbation.

Presently Vance walked in, which gave me an excuse to break into Daryl's erotic monologue. I stood up as he saw me and came over to shake hands and welcome me back. I introduced him to Daryl and they shook hands in that measuring way I was beginning to recognize, the one that says, "can I take this guy?"

I invited him to sit down, but he looked at his watch and said, "It's getting close to eight, we'd better get next door." He seemed to feel no need to use military time; maybe he'd never been in the military. I realized I didn't know. "The master of ceremonies doesn't like to be kept waiting," he elaborated with a small smile.

"The master of -"

He laughed. "MC," he said, "Mac. It is a joke."

"I'm not up on all the jokes yet," I said.

"This briefing is no joke, however. Mac is not the joking kind." The three of us walked out the door to go around to the opposite entrance. As at a signal, the others got up to follow us. We all found seats and sat there until, precisely at eight o'clock - twenty hundred hours to be militarily correct - Mac walked in, looking just the same as he had the day before. Even the suit looked the same, although I doubted it was the same one. No one could stay that neat after a long plane and car ride.

Still relatively fresh from OTS, I started to stand up as we were taught to do when a superior officer enters a briefing room. Vance put a restraining arm on my shoulder, saving me from the small embarrassment suffered by two others who did stand briefly before looking around in confusion and sitting down again. Mac didn't crack a smile.

"Gentlemen - and lady," he nodded in the direction of the lone girl in the room. "You are about to start a training program - at least continue one - which is unique in America's history. While working with the military, we are actually operating apart from it and will dispense with the military formalities. I am called Mac, not sir, and the same goes for your instructors, Frank, Vance, Abraham, Fedder and Rasmussen." He pointed to each in turn. I looked at each one as he named them, congratulating myself on identifying them as instructors in the canteen. A couple, Frank and Abraham especially, looked older than the rest of us, but they, as well as the others, stood out somehow. I'm not sure quite why, other than all of them seemed to have a "finished" look - and don't ask me what *that* means.

Mac was continuing, "Frank will be your surveillance and interrogation instructor. Vance, here, will conduct small arms and hand-to-hand training, a continuation of your earlier education. Abraham will take you through the intricacies of codes, ciphers and similar intelligence skills. Fedder will teach you about explosives, Rasmussen about the more exotic forms of mayhem and together they will show you how to perform with a partner. I will occasionally be here to add to your education as best I can."

I was disappointed that he didn't mention rifle, knife and fencing training, not that I felt I needed them, but I was still young and naive enough to want to show off. I got my chance sooner than I thought.

"There is one change in our faculty. Vance, who normally also teaches rifle and knife classes, has informed me that you would be better served with a different instructor. So, one of our students here, Eric, will take over those classes."

I started to look around before I realized he meant *me*! I was shocked and immensely flattered all at once. I also remembered Vance's comment on not being too proud to use an expert and realized it was practiced all the way to the top. I think it was at that point that I really *knew* I had found a home. I caught Vance's eye and nodded to him in thanks. He nodded back with an amused look. I refrained from looking at any of the other students.

Mac said dryly, "I take it from your expression, Eric, that Vance did not tell you as I asked him to. Well, Vance does like his little jokes." Addressing the rest of the class, he continued, "Although Eric is the first of you to perform as an instructor, I sincerely hope he will not be the last. In this unit, we will need every resource we can get. Whenever any of you displays a special talent, if you can teach it to the others, you'll be asked to do so."

Thus expertly smoothing over any ruffled feelings, he continued, "This assignment has taken you out of the mainstream of the war, but it's still a war of sorts and you can consider yourselves still soldiers of a sort, but I'd rather you wouldn't. Don't make up any pretty mental pictures. If you were working for a criminal organization, you'd be known as enforcers. Since you're working for a sovereign nation, you can call yourselves ... well, "removers" is a very good word. It describes the job with reasonable accuracy."

Mac always did have a knack at getting to the heart of the matter. We were all instantly sobered, which I would imagine was his intent. I had always thought of myself as rather cold-blooded, but this guy had me beat in spades.

"You are being given a thorough course of training, courtesy of Uncle Sam. It's possible that Uncle, being a peaceful sort, wouldn't approve of everything in the curriculum, but what Uncle doesn't know won't hurt him. Security has its advantages, and we're very top-secret here. We're supposed to be developing some kind of a mystery weapon, I believe. Well, one might call it that.

After all, the greatest mystery on earth, and the most dangerous weapon, is man himself.

"During your training here you are going to be taught many skills which, for obvious reasons, cannot be practiced fully - at least if we want you all to survive the course - as it is not practical to provide victims upon which to practice."

I heard a low chuckle somewhere behind me, but I was watching Mac's eyes and could see no hint that he was joking - I got the impression that the cold-blooded bastard would have not hesitated to "provide victims" if he thought he could have gotten away with it. I'm not criticizing, mind you; it *would* have made our training more effective.

Completely deadpan, he continued, "There is also a certain amount of training that has to do with mental conditioning which cannot be practiced at all. We simply pound it into your heads and hope it takes. Each profession has its rules of engagement and code of conduct; however in ours, the penalties for lapses are unusually severe and often fatal.

"Rule one," he held up his index finger. "The mission takes precedence. We will not knowingly send you on a suicide mission, but if your success requires your death or the death of another - including your comrades or even innocent bystanders - that is regrettable, but necessary. We are at war, after all, and our missions will most likely be necessary to save many other lives." There were several nods around the room. This was standard military procedure, although I had my doubts about the veracity of his suicide mission comment.

"Rule two. *You* are not expendable, except when it conflicts with rule one. We will have a considerable amount of time, effort and money tied up in each one of you. After your mission is successfully completed, your only concern is to return alive, regardless of the breakage. If you are captured alive, you will make every attempt to escape. There is one exception to this rule that brings us to rule three:

"The first thing you are taught in the military is the axiom that you must not tell the enemy anything other than name, rank and serial number, if captured. In this unit, that nonsense does not apply. With enough time and effort, anyone can be forced to talk. If you have potentially dangerous information in your head - a situation we will make every attempt to avoid - you are expected to avoid being taken alive and a means to that end will be provided to each of you." He paused a moment as we absorbed that idea.

"Other than that, you are free to say anything you wish, to avoid torture that might render you unable to escape. I hope that's clear to everyone. Unlike the movies, I have found that a smart, scheming coward generally outlives the brave, courageous hero who laughs in the face of danger and stupidly does or says precisely the wrong thing and gets himself shot. Not that I'm implying anyone here is a coward; there's just a time to act cowardly and a time to act brave and I hope - for your sakes - that you learn the difference."

I had no particular problem with this philosophy but I could tell from the fidgeting that one or two of the others were having a hard time with it. Well, what do you expect from a generation brought up on the exploits of Clark Gable and Errol Flynn and Gary Cooper? Mac seemed determined to hit us with everything at once. I wondered if everyone would still be here tomorrow.

He wasn't done yet. "Rule four. We don't play the hostage game, ever, in all its permutations. If your target grabs someone as a shield, simply shoot through the two of them. If your partner is captured and your surrender is demanded, you don't. Period. No matter whom is held hostage for your behavior, we … don't … play … that … game. When in doubt, see rules one and two. That is not to mean that rescue attempts are not allowed - quite the contrary so long as the mission is not jeopardized."

He didn't bother to pause. By now he probably figured - correctly - that we were all pretty numb. "Rule five, and the final rule. No one dies in vain. If you're betrayed you are expected to remove the betrayer if at all possible. If someone feeds you a Mickey Finn or poison and is stupid enough to hang around to see you pass out or die, you will assume that person is not a friend of yours and take appropriate action, preferably fatal. If you find yourself in a position - quite possible, even likely - where your death is imminent, I expect you to die with your gun empty, your knives used and your grenades expended, and as many dead bodies around you that it is humanly - or inhumanly - possible to accomplish. Any questions?"

He waited for a moment but there were no takers. "Good. I'm not one to spend a lot of time discussing philosophy, but I feel quite strongly about this next point. You've all heard the rumors coming out of Germany and its subjugated countries. Mass murder, genocide and atrocities of all kinds. Actually, from what I've learned, the rumors only scratch the surface.

It's the modern dilemma. It would be simply marvelous if the human animal weren't aggressive by nature, so a lot of people figure they can stop it from being so just by having everybody pretend it isn't so. The only trouble is, they won't sit down and calculate what's going to happen if the prescription doesn't work on everybody who takes it.

"What happens is that arrogant thugs start shoving people around, serenely confident that none of their brainwashed, nonviolent fellow-citizens will be willing to, or able to, lift a hand in effective self-defense. Once you start raising whole generations on the lovely, unrealistic principle that the use of force is always evil and unthinkable, that you should be willing to endure any indignity and pay any price rather than spill a little blood, why, you've set yourself right up for them. For the intimidators. For the people who haven't the slightest qualms about using force or spilling blood. For the ones on whom the pretend-we're-all-nice medicine didn't work. All the bullies and dictators and little-league Caesars. And a big-league monster named Hitler.

"I doubt that there's ever been a war in history where the good and bad sides have been so clearly defined. However, regardless of my

43

feelings - or yours - on the subject, you have my word that I will never accept a mission designed to target someone solely because he's a vicious bastard. It would be too hard to draw the line, and sometimes it's hard to tell. All of our targets will be determined from a military or security viewpoint - what will further our military objective, save lives or protect vital information - and if the target is otherwise a nice, friendly, warm human being, that's just too bad. That is the reason this unit was formed and the reason for the rules.

"Just keep in mind that we are serving an important role. Don't hate the enemy - it clouds your judgment and it is a waste of time and energy. It is only necessary to kill him."

Chapter 7

The next day we started in earnest. There were no more secrets, no pretenses. We were being trained to kill, efficiently and by any means available. Every other part of the training was a means to an end. We had to learn how to stay alive, of course, to survive long enough to make the touch - that was the word used in our outfit, why I don't know - and we had to learn how to disengage and make it back home. Along the way we might have to indulge in some secret-agent stuff, including interrogation, but most of that was handled in the classroom. In the field, we concentrated on killing.

I was surprised that no one defected. There wasn't much talking that first day and you could sense the mental wheels spinning, but each of us seemed to have come to terms with the implications of Mac's little speech the night before. I suppose that was the purpose of the speech. I never again heard him talk at that length on any non-job-related subject.

Except for special night training, our days were regulated in a typical military fashion, with one major exception. No more PT - physical training for you non-military types. I halfway expected to fall out in the morning for jumping jacks, push-ups, mile runs and all the other nonsense designed to make an otherwise healthy human being ache and hurt and wish he'd picked another profession. Not that we didn't get plenty of exercise, but it was specific exercise, as in hand-to-hand combat, fencing and jumping for cover when a grenade landed too close for comfort.

We also didn't have a lot of nonsense about our personal habits. If you had a hand free and wanted a cigarette, you just lit up. There were times I could have used one myself - or my old pipe - but I had given up the habit when it got to be a nuisance around the darkroom. In that youthful, pre-war period of my life, I'd carried a big 4x5 Speed Graphic camera like a shining sword and worn a press pass in my hat like reporters do in the movies - at least I did until I was laughed out of it by the reporters on the paper. They'd called me Flashbulb Helm, thanks to an instant christening by Frank McKenna. He was one of those ageless, pink, chubby, baby-faced characters who remember everybody they've ever met and are always glad to see them. I don't know why. Personally, I've met a lot of people I'd just as soon forget. Nobody had ever called him Frank. He'd been universally known as Buddy and had been one of the people who'd laughed me out of my pretentious stage and set me on the path to becoming a reasonably competent journalist.

Anyway, I'd found that you simply couldn't get a clear, crisp print in a darkroom filled with smoke and had gradually quit smoking altogether. But I still liked a drink occasionally, and was pleased to discover that even hard liquor was available after the evening meal, although consumed in limited quantities - you didn't want to be nursing a hangover when Vance worked you over with his version of Karate. Mac, if it was his idea, took care of his people and those who didn't particularly like beer - I was in that category - found their favorite tipple well stocked. That's what I call a thorough background check.

Most of the field training was designed not just to refine our physical skills, but to teach us the concepts that distinguish the highly competent amateur from the true professional. For example, we had drilled into us the simple fact that a man aiming a gun at you was a hostile act demanding instant and violent retaliation whenever possible. A man who aims a gun at you is a man who can kill you, and you don't want to leave people like that standing around. A gun is a gun and a threat is a threat, and we were trained to react first and do our heavy thinking later. Like savage dogs, we were taught to go for the throat when threatened.

I remember the way Vance put it. "A gun is serious business. Once you point a gun at somebody you're a murderer; whether or not you get around to pulling the trigger is irrelevant. So you'd damn well better decide if that's what you want before you start waving the piece around. It's only in the movies that a pistol, or whatever, is a magic wand that bends people peacefully to your will. The cops have to try it because they're supposed to bring 'em back alive if they can. We don't. I don't point guns at people I'm not prepared to kill; and if anybody points a gun at me, I figure he means it, and I think about nothing but killing him until I have him totally dead. Or he has me; but somehow that hasn't happened yet. Forget that idiot drop-your-gun-and-put-your-hands-up nonsense. The moment you aim a gun at somebody, you've moved into the killing zone and you'd better be ready to finish the job and do them in fast before they do you."

As I've indicated, I'd grown up with guns, knowing perfectly well that a firearm is simply a tool for drilling a small round hole in an object, inanimate or animate. If that's what you want, fine; but don't expect a little .22 or even a roaring, thundering .45 to turn you into some kind of omnipotent deity with absolute control of the world around you. You might end up dying in a spreading puddle of blood and urine, staring up at your killer reproachfully, wondering why he hadn't got the word that a gun was all it would take to make you a big man giving orders to everybody. I think that's the reason Mac liked hunters, people like me. The hardest thing to teach someone who hasn't grown up with guns is not *how* to shoot but *when* to shoot.

Vance also had something to say on that subject. "If you're facing someone who knows guns, he's not going to just fold up and become a meek little prisoner, like in the movies. There's only one answer to the old empty-gun gambit. It's that same as for the look-out-there's-somebody-behind-you routine. You just pull the damn trigger. You may wind up with a dead man on the floor, but there's a better chance of its not being you.

"The same thing holds true when you're faced with more than one professional. The standard procedure is to start moving slowly apart, shuffling their feet, not really enough to be threatening, just enough to finally make their move when you can no longer adequately cover all of them. If you hesitate, you're dead. Don't waste your breath on useless threats - they'll know you don't mean it. Just shoot the first one who moves and the others will behave themselves. Usually," he added with a wolfish grin.

Most of us learned quickly, if we hadn't already known most of it. But Stella - the only girl in the group - apparently hadn't had the same gun-orientated background as the rest of us. Well, maybe Mac had chosen her using different criteria. She listened, but you could tell it was a foreign language to her and while she learned to shoot, she had a hard time even with the basics. You always check a gun after it's handed to you - or received through other, less peaceful means - even if you think you know it's loaded. Or unloaded. Vance used the standard trick of range instructors, appearing to be loading a weapon while actually palming the cartridges, and handed it to Stella. She took it, aimed at the target, and attempted to fire the unloaded weapon in full view of the rest of us. I don't think she ever really forgave Vance and was cool to him from then on, but that was the last time she forgot to check a weapon - at least on the range. In the field, a lot of otherwise intelligent agents died by forgetting this principle and I always wondered if that was what happened to her a few months later. She was the first of our little group to die in the field, but not the last.

When it came time for rifle training, not to be outdone, I had my share of things to teach the rest of the group. Whether you're hunting animals or people with a telescope-mounted rifle, the principle is the same. My lecture went like this:

"The best way to fluff a difficult shot is to think too much about it. Oh, advance planning and preparation are necessary, of course: The gun must be properly tuned and sighted, and the ammunition must be carefully loaded unless you're willing to settle for the lesser accuracy of the factory product - perfectly reliable, of course, but in the nature of things it can never be tailored to the characteristics of your particular rifle. The target area must be inspected to make certain that no twigs or branches will intervene to deflect the bullet. The firing point must be selected with care, and a steady rest provided. The probable wind conditions must be studied; and a table of allowances must be prepared for various wind velocities. The range must, of course, be determined with care, although, with a powerful, flat-shooting weapon you do have some leeway. If you're shooting on a slant, the range must, of course, be the horizontal distance to your target, not the slant distance. Gravity does not operate in a slanting direction; bullet drop does not depend upon the slant distance to the target but only upon the horizontal component thereof; so on long shots you have to hold under to allow for this.

"But once all this has been done, the thinking must stop. In particular, all clever last-minute brainstorms, adjustments, inspirations, and corrective impulses must be strangled at birth.

"I still remember, very clearly, my first shot at an antelope. I was a boy, hunting with my father; and there was the dream buck we'd been looking for. But he looked so *small* compared to the mule deer I'd already hunted successfully! The mental computer went into action unbidden: Looking so small, he must be very far away, best to hold over a bit to allow for the drop of the bullet at that great range. So I shot high, and missed high; and it was another two years before I finally bagged an antelope, not nearly as spectacular as that one. Actually, the target had looked small simply because the pronghorn is a small animal. A dead-center hold such as Dad had carefully instructed me to use would have got me that trophy - the first one lost to me by excessive cerebration, but not the last."

I don't know how much they learned that was new to them, but they listened attentively enough, with those too-polite expressions that said I wasn't really an instructor, just one of them, even if I did know about rifles. That was okay with me, I hadn't asked for the job anyway. At least they didn't laugh, and Vance, standing at the back, gave me the "OK" sign with his thumb and forefinger. To be honest, I kind of enjoyed the experience.

As near as I could determine, all the instructors were hell-on-wheels in all aspects of the business - if business was the right word to describe what we were doing - but each had his own specialty or specialties. When not teaching these specialties to the group, they were as likely as not to show up at one of the other classes and most of them attended mine. It gave me a lot of respect for Mac's ability to choose people. I think we all learned more because of the example set by the instructors, not to mention making my debut easier - if the instructors were interested in what I had to say, then perhaps my classmates should give me a chance. . . .

Often I found myself wondering where the instructors had acquired their experience. I mean, I understand the mechanical skills with firearms and edged weapons, and I suppose that the hand-to-hand stuff has a certain peacetime following. But some of the more exotic skills and especially the depth of knowledge going beyond the physical to the mental expertise, I couldn't figure. We'd been at peace for a relatively long time, so where did Mac find some of these people?

Take Frank for instance. I'd seen him twice before taking his interrogation class. The second time he'd been fairly friendly, but he'd been in a car and I'd only really noticed him in profile, so to speak. Sitting in his class was a different experience. He looked quite ordinary. They usually do. Very few of them have werewolf fangs and pointed, tufted ears. He was dressed in a faded, flowery sports shirt, frayed jeans, and tennis shoes. But I didn't like his eyes. Well, hell, maybe he didn't like mine. We all have our little specialties. I was in no position to criticize, even though I was just a little uncomfortable - it's one thing to kill a man; it's quite another to torture him. Frank had just explained the concept of the I-Team - "I" being short for interrogation, of course - that was being formed in London to handle certain prisoners who had vital information we needed. My conscience - what was left of it - told me that if I had to get information by such means the least I could do was to get my own hands bloody. Using an I-team would make me like the kind of hypocritical creep who loves steak but wouldn't dream of going out and murdering a poor little steer - or deer - himself. Or herself.

Apparently with that same thought in mind, Frank was explaining the basic principle behind interrogation techniques. "Dignity," he said. "Remember that dignity is the key to any man's resistance, or any woman's. As long as your subject is allowed to feel that he's still a human being with rights and privileges and self-respect, he can usually hold out indefinitely. Take, for instance, a soldier in a clean uniform, lead him politely to a desk, seat him decorously on a chair, request him to place his hands before him, stick splinters under his fingernails, and set fire to them ... and you'll be surprised how often he'll watch his fingertips cooking and laugh in your face. But if you take the same man, first, and work him over to show that you don't mind bruising your knuckles and don't have a bit of respect for his integrity as a man - you don't have to hurt him much, just mess him up until he can no longer cling to a romanticized picture of himself as a noble and handsome embodiment of stubborn courage."

Like I said, I wondered where Frank got his training. Or Mac himself. We had lots of fun discussing Mac. One school of thought had it that although he was great at picking, and setting up training programs for, dangerous men, Mac himself couldn't fight his way out of a lightweight airmail envelope. I didn't buy it. Nobody got that look sitting behind a desk, and I've often thought about his possible background. He wasn't really old enough to have gotten that much experience in the first war - what up to now had always been called The Great War. I had in mind a certain little-known arm of British intelligence, not that Mac was even remotely British, but they were known to hire Americans upon occasion. Or perhaps he'd been one of those soldiers-of-fortune so popular in the movies. Hell, he could have been an enforcer for Al Capone or one of the New York Families, recruited out of prison just for this purpose, but that didn't wash. I'm not sure why, but I had the impression that this idea was his own little baby from start to finish and he'd had to work like hell to sell the idea to someone.

Mac kind of appeared and disappeared at random. I assumed he had other duties involving the first group to graduate from the Ranch. When he was in residence, so to speak, he taught an occasional class himself. One of the more interesting ones had to do with escape. He covered a lot of ground on basic techniques, but the part that stuck in my mind, and saved my life a time or two, was his lecture on escape theory.

51

He didn't pull any punches or dress it up in fancy language. And, to me at least, it sounded like he was speaking from experience, not just theory. "In the movies," he explained, "you see the heroes - and heroines - carefully plotting their escape, planning a way to break out, overpower their captors, tie them up nice and neat, and summon help, preferably with a minimum of bloodshed, being the nice movie heroes they are. That's dream stuff. The basic principle of escaping is that there is no problem in escaping, none whatever, if everyone who's in a position to prevent you from escaping has been killed. To turn a phrase, you go for the throats, not the boats. Never mind that Gustav's been reasonably polite, to date. Never mind that Max's attitude is understandable or that Heinrich may have something to be said in his favor also. You just forget all that. If you get a chance to use a knife, it must go in all the way, low, edge up, and rip upward until it hits bone. Then you step back fast and let the guts spill out, filling the air with that nasty stench you get when you dress out a deer or an elk carelessly and damage the intestines, letting the contents of the digestive tract spill out. If you get chance to swing some kind of blunt instrument, there should be brains on it when you stop swinging. Forget all about trying to escape. Escape will take care of itself, later. As long as there's one of them standing, moving, even twitching slightly, you keep after him and to hell with escape. Too damned many people, thinking about getting away instead of concentrating on the job at hand, have been killed at the last moment by somebody they chivalrously refrained from finishing off when they had the chance, movie fashion. You don't want to die because you were too sensitive to give somebody who was still wiggling another bash on the head, and he managed to reach a gun before he died."

To me, that is the sound of experience. In college, most of my professors had only been teachers, not doers. When they taught a class it was with a certain amount of abstraction; theory, not practice, if you know what I mean. But my photojournalism professor had spent twenty-five years on the job before retiring to teach. His class came alive and when he explained how to frame a subject you *knew* he had done it, and not just once. This training had the same flavor. Every one of our instructors had been there

52

and done it. I think because of that, I listened with just a little more attention than I might have otherwise - which is probably why I survived the war.

Take this example from Rassmussen. I think we caught him in an off moment, because he left a definite impression of prior experience and a wider knowledge of his fellow instructors than we had. I'm not even sure how the discussion got started. I think someone asked him about getting out after a job was finished. He looked at the recruit - I believe it was Karl, a dark-haired, wiry man of German descent, who spoke flawless German and, as I remember, gave me a run for my money with the sabers - and hesitated for an instant before answering. "It comes down to learning to play the odds, assuming you have a choice. For example, if you're being chased in a car by a guy behind who is definitely trying to kill you, and there's probably some other guys at a roadblock not too far ahead who'd also like to kill you, you've got to get away fast. You can't be bothered with the minor statistical possibility of meeting a stranger on a blind curve with you on the wrong side of the road. It's one of the lesser risks, let's say.

"On the other hand, when you've got your back to the wall you don't waste time figuring the odds. If your life is at stake, you just blow away the guy in front of you and grab his weapon if yours is going dry and start walking and keep firing. Eventually you're either out of there or dead. And if you're dead, they'll remember you, those who're left standing. They'll remember how hard you were to put down, and how many you took down with you; and maybe they won't be quite so eager to tackle the next guy from your outfit who comes along. We call it public relations. We're a bunch of screwballs. Certain things were left out of us, or trained out of us, or beaten out of us. Like a normal reverence for human life, and that includes our own human lives. In other words, we were taught that if we gotta go, well, we gotta go; let's just see how much company we can take to hell with us."

While he had been talking, I was visualizing the situation, feeling I'd been there with him. You don't get that feeling from someone who is only teaching theory. There was a brief silence before he continued with the class, when I had the distinct feeling that he had not so much been talking to us as he'd been remembering lost comrades in another place.

And speaking of Karl, he'd been the second of our group to be promoted to instructor status. We spent the entire time brushing up on our German, both in formal classes, which Karl had been quickly drafted to teach, in the field and in our spare time. We'd all been exposed to German at one time or another - apparently that was another criterion Mac used - and were all fluent by the time we graduated. It was what you could call an essential part of working undercover in Germany, or German-occupied territory. We also practiced French and Italian. I'd had German and French in college, pretty much standard with journalism majors, and could speak pretty good Spanish after growing up in New Mexico. As I've previously indicated, I also learned Swedish from my parents, after a fashion. But I seemed to have a mental block when it came to Italian - maybe it was too close to Spanish and I got confused. In any case, Mac never sent me to Italy - I spent the entire war in England, France and Germany.

There were occasional fights, but those were broken up fairly quickly by the instructors at first, and by the rest of us as our training progressed - we were getting too skilled at murder and mayhem to allow a fight to go much beyond the pushing and swinging stage. Somebody could die. Toward the end of the course, we'd pretty much worked out all the petty disagreements and could live with one another - self control was high on the list of subjects taught.

There was one other subject taught during the course. It was considered the most important and wasn't so much a class as an ongoing harassment - my word, not theirs. It was called preparedness or alertness or some such title. The way it was done was this: you'd be walking innocently between buildings at the school, or having a beer at the canteen, and you'd be chatting with an off-duty instructor in a friendly manner. Suddenly, smiling, patting you on the back and telling you what a swell guy you were and how he'd never had a pupil like you, he'd produce an unloaded gun and shove it in your side. At least you hoped the gun was unloaded. At that place you were never quite sure. And it wasn't just the instructors; it could be the guy you bunked with, or the pretty girl at the canteen. Your job was to react and react fast, even if it was Mac himself. If you wasted any time in conversation, you flunked the course.

We'd been taught how to break a strangle-hold, either with a smashing upward drive of both arms - hands locked together - or finger by finger. Somehow, the classroom training made it seem perfectly logical and relatively easy ... until someone snuck into your room at night and grabbed you by the neck. The combination of sleep fog and instant unadulterated terror drove home the lesson in a way classroom training would never do.

It made for an interesting, if stressful, two months...

Chapter 8

There's a big mystique associated with seamanship. If you weren't born in a forecastle in the middle of a hurricane and didn't cut your teeth on a marlinespike, you'll never qualify. Well, hell, they told me just about the same thing about horses when I was a kid. The fact is, there are people with vested interests in just about every sport who get a big kick out of making their particular athletic activity seem too difficult for ordinary mortals to comprehend, let alone master. I've been known to tell beginners how hard it is to shoot straight, myself. Actually, making a boat or horse go where you want it to, or making a gun go bang in approximately the right direction, isn't all that tough once you've decided not to let the experts intimidate you. Sailing, however, seems to attract an inordinate share of these unforgiving experts. You've got to call everything by the right name or the damn boat will sink like a rock. At least that's the impression I got from the dockside geniuses.

We had been sent to Annapolis for a two-week course in small-boat handling for spooks who might be put ashore on strange coasts and were learning to do things the Navy way, on the water, at least.

We'd each been given a two-week leave before reporting to Annapolis. I'd spent part of mine in Albuquerque with an old friend - well, girlfriend - who was willing to overlook our last disagreement. She hadn't appreciated, nor understood, my sudden decision to join the Army. She thought it was just terrible that men had to kill each other and why did I have to stoop to that level? I think Kathy also had other plans for me which involved a ring and a church, but that was strictly a one-way proposition. I avoided the subject as much as possible to keep the peace, but anyone who calmly eats meat of any kind while railing against the hunters who kill those poor animals is not going to figure much in my long-range plans - especially matrimony.

I always swore that the first time I met a girl with smoke still curling up from the barrel of her rifle, a hunting knife in her hand and blood up to her elbows from dressing out her kill, I would propose on the spot. I knew there was at least one like that out there somewhere. My life would have been a cruel joke if there wasn't. Meanwhile, while I was waiting for my dream girl, simple biology played its own jokes on me. I seemed to be constantly getting involved with otherwise intelligent females who looked at me in horror when I insisted on my annual hunting trip. You'd think I would have found one who, although not sharing my interests to the point of joining me, would at least be tolerant enough to indulge my infrequent forays into the wilds. The closest I ever came was one who condescended to join me on a fishing trip, but refused to touch a worm or a fresh-caught fish. She was, however, perfectly willing to eat the fish after I did the necessary preliminary work, including the cooking.

I'll admit I don't understand this aversion on the part of the current female population to harm an animal which, for thousands of years, had provided sustenance to their ancestors. It seemed to me we were breeding most of the survival instincts out of the human race. I can't remember anything that startled me more than one episode during training. I'd found myself being attracted to Stella, despite her attire. Well, the fact that she was the only female in sight might have had something to do with it - I'm human, regardless of some opinions to the contrary. She might have been inexperienced with firearms, but put a blade or a garrote in her hands and she was sudden death. She got carried away in one practice session and damn near strangled me when I failed to get my hand between the loop and my neck. She was concentrating so much that Rasmussen, the instructor for the class, had to stop her before she did some permanent damage. She immediately apologized and, far from being upset, I was looking at her with a new respect.

Later that night, a few of us were sitting around the canteen, discussing various hunting experiences. Stella came by and I half-jokingly - if she'd accepted I would have gladly followed through - suggested she join me in a deer-hunting trip after training to give her some practice with a real live target. She looked at me in astonishment and coldly stated, "I would never kill an innocent animal!"

I thought she was joking back at first until I saw the look on her face. She was actually disgusted with the thought of killing a deer, but apparently had no qualms - witness my sore neck - about strangling a fellow human being. I'd met several hunters who had serious problems with killing humans, and even thought the death penalty was immoral, but this was the first time I'd run into the reverse. I had obviously been born in the wrong century. At least I wasn't alone. The guys sitting with me seemed almost as flabbergasted as I was. That effectively killed any further ideas I had concerning any kind of amorous relationship with Stella.

Anyway, between Stella and my long abstinence, the pressure had been building up, so to speak, and Kathy looked pretty good to me. She'd decided to forgive me and give me a proper send-off to war. It was nice for a while, and biology is a fairly reliable source of motivation, but when you've run with the wolves you kind of lose interest in cocker spaniels, bright and docile and well-trained though they may be. A few days before my leave was up, I told her goodbye and headed up in the mountains for a fishing trip with a rented pick-up and a small motorboat. I figured to get in a little practice with small boats and indulge myself - I didn't think I'd get a chance to do much fishing again for quite a while.

I arrived at Annapolis, rested, confident and relatively free of sexual tension. I was looking forward to the small-boat training. Imagine my surprise… To me, living in the land-locked southwest, a small boat was a twelve-foot rowboat with an anemic little trolling motor attached as opposed, say, to an eighteen-footer with twin outboards. These guys measured small on a scale that included destroyers, carriers and cruisers.

We spent the first three days in a classroom, looking at pictures and memorizing the names of things - our instructor was one of those who insisted on the right terminology before he would allow us aboard. Finally we loaded up in a military bus and headed for the dock. There were seven of us from Mac's outfit, along with an assortment of shady-looking characters from - I assumed, since they weren't talking any more than we were - some other undercover agencies. Two of our group - Gene and Derek, if it matters - had been recruited from the Navy and had graduated from Annapolis, rendering small-boat training a tad redundant. The two of them, together with Charles, an Army Air Corps pilot - the code name probably came from Lindbergh, given Mac's dry sense of humor - had the slightly pompous sense of self-importance which seems to be prevalent - not to mention irritating to the rest of us - among people who have developed highly-specialized skills, especially skills involving large killing machines. In fairness, I suppose I sounded fairly pompous myself when teaching the others the finer points of the three-hundred yard shot from a prone rest. By now, I guess you're beginning to get the idea that we're not noted for brotherhood and companionship and esprit de corps and you're right. In the more traditional armed forces, they've got discipline. It must be nice. All we've got is temperament.

We got off the bus, accompanied by our instructor and two midshipmen who had been hastily recruited to repair our mistakes before they got fatal - well I understand that overturning a sailboat is not necessarily a disaster as they don't sink without a lot of help, but I've never felt that strongly about my swimming abilities. I'm built all wrong and tend to sink like a rock if I stop moving. My dad had tried to teach me something called the "dead man's float", a nomenclature that, had I relied upon the technique, would have been more literal than descriptive.

The boat was up on shore when we first saw her, as part of our training was to get her in the water. Why we needed that particular talent, I don't know. I suppose that, as usual, Mac had been less than totally honest as to how the training was to be put to use, and they had assumed we were to learn everything there was to know about sailing, including the manual labor part of it. Twenty-eight feet long on deck, with a bowsprit adding another couple of feet, she was sandwiched in between two larger and racier powerboats that made her look quite small, but sturdy and seaworthy, by comparison. The mast seemed very tall, however. The name on the transom was *Betty*, which seemed rather unoriginal.

Setting sail is, I believe, supposed to be a five-minute job on a boat the size of *Betty*. It took us well over two hours. All the lines seemed to go to the wrong places, and if they were correctly led, we found them tangled in the rigging overhead when we tried to haul on them. The mast was equipped with a rope ladder, so you could climb up to fix things at the top, but then the ladder seemed to have a devilish affinity for any rope that flopped within range. Nothing worked right the first time, or even the second, but at last we had the little sail hoisted forward of the mast and the big one hoisted aft of it, reasonably taut and pretty. Actually I think they're called the forestaysail and the mainsail, respectively, but I won't guarantee it.

We sped out of the harbor at a gentle two knots with an occasional surge to three. Hardly America's cup performance, but good enough for a few landlubbers feeling their cautious way toward seamanship. Once we got far enough out, they had us break out the real stuff, something called a Genoa jib, affectionately known as Jenny. With *Betty* pitching gently in the slow swells, we had to crawl out onto the precarious bowsprit - my job, naturally - and set the giant as it flapped wildly. It took an hour to get the big sail up and organized to our instructor's satisfaction. Finally we had to tidy up the foredeck and bring down the little forestaysail and roll it neatly again, because, he said after careful study, it was too small to pull worth a damn under the conditions and it disturbed the wind for Jenny. Taking the helm himself, he had us crank in a bit on this winch and ease that sheet a touch - it took fifteen minutes more before he pronounced himself satisfied with all adjustments.

It's the great sailboat fallacy, as far as I'm concerned. It's a pleasant way of getting around on the water, it's nice and quiet, and the wind is free although the sails damn well aren't; but fast it isn't, so why not just relax and glide along at three knots instead of beating your brains out to make three and a quarter? Then I decided that this was the wrong attitude. After all, it was a useful educational experience for me, and the others seemed to be enjoying it, so why spoil the fun? With this attitude, I was able to enjoy the rest of the course and actually learned something. By graduation time, I could handle the boat as well as the rest of them, so long as I was left alone to do the job and not remember the damn names of everything, a particularly snobbish attitude for a guy who gets upset whenever someone refers to a cartridge as a bullet.

The last day, we enjoyed the full U.S. Naval Academy Band giving Sousa hell as the midshipmen passed in review on the banks of the Severn. It was a stirring sight; however, I gave thanks to whatever impulse prompted me to join the Army, a hell of an attitude given my Viking ancestry.

Chapter 9

We flew to London via military transport, in uniform and carrying orders and ID cards which looked real. Well, I suppose they were. It's not considered counterfeiting if you use real forms with official seals. The fact that the unit assignments and specialty descriptions were false didn't make them less real. And, on the small chance that anybody checked, there were real records back in Washington which backed up the orders and IDs.

I wasn't sure whether or not to be happy about flying rather than sailing across the Atlantic. On the one hand, flying was faster, thus making my discomfort shorter. However, I was about ten times more scared of flying than sailing, so I guess things evened out. Given a choice, I would prefer to drive but the last I heard, there were no bridges spanning the Atlantic. Everybody's got their own hang-ups - heights and depths were mine - and the fact that I was happier doing a hundred and fifty miles an hour on a racetrack in a souped-up hot rod, rather than flying or sailing, didn't seem at all inconsistent to me.

I once knew a guy who'd cheerfully climb a vertical mountain cliff with a mile of empty space below him and only a rope and a few long nails - I think they're called pitons - between him and certain death. He called it a hobby. He also climbed stairs - he was scared to death of elevators or any other enclosed space. I've also heard of lion-tamers who were afraid of snakes. The next time you feel like criticizing someone for an unreasonable fear, remember that the victim knows it's unreasonable, but just can't help it. He just has to learn to live with it. That's the way I am about planes. I know that it's silly, that the safety record for planes is much better than for automobiles but I still grip the armrests until my knuckles turn white on take-offs and landings and, when given a choice, always opt for an aisle seat, preferably over a wing.

This was the longest flight I'd had to date and the only way I got through it was to sleep most of the time. That's my greatest talent.

I can usually sleep anytime and anywhere, given half a chance. Once we landed, I limped off the plane painfully - those seats were not really made for sleeping, especially when your legs are a full foot longer than the space provided for them.

Vance was there to meet us, which surprised me at first. Later, he explained that each group of instructors stayed with one class all the way into the field. That made sense after I thought about it. It provided continuity of training, while ensuring that no one instructor knew too many of Mac's agents, for security reasons. It also made me wonder who could take over in the event something happened to Mac, but I decided it didn't matter - without Mac there *was* no group.

We got everything loaded and took off in the dark - daylight had come and gone while we were in the air, with the sun disappearing as we landed. As London was blacked out, we had no idea where we were going. Three hours later we arrived, were greeted by the rest of the instructors, off-loaded and assigned sleeping quarters, with orders to meet in the cafeteria next to the hangar at oh seven hundred.

Morning came damned early - we were several hours ahead of Washington time and a couple more ahead of Arizona time. As I stumbled into the cafeteria looking for the coffee pot I was thankful for the sleep I'd had on the plane. From their looks, my companions were in worse shape than I was - apparently they had been unable - or unwilling - to sleep during the flight over. I sat down next to Nick, feeling he was the least likely to try conversation. I was right. He just nodded to me and continued with his breakfast. He was one of the icy ones, and in a way I envied him; he'd never have to worry about getting overly friendly with someone he'd been assigned to work with or protect - or shoot. He wouldn't think about philosophies and emotions and feelings. It was the safe and professional way to handle it. But ice is pretty brittle, and he'd crack some day; the cold ones always do. But that was in the future. Right now he was the right man for the job. In training, he was efficient and helpful and courteous, but always aloof. Right now I appreciated that quality.

I looked down at his breakfast eggs and felt my stomach turn. I decided to finish my coffee before trying anything else. I wasn't the only one. Besides Nick, only the instructors were eating, over at a table by themselves. Everyone else still had that far-away stare that only comes from lack of sleep. Eventually a few of us tried some pastries, leaving the eggs to congeal. They were excellent and our spirits perked up a bit.

The door opened and Mac walked in, looking fresh, well-rested and well-fed. I assumed he ate food like the rest of us, but had seen no evidence of it yet. He wasn't much for off-duty fraternization. He was still dressed like a banker. "Welcome to London," he said. "Or at least close to it. You'll see London in a few days, but for now, we have a treat for you. Now that your basic training is out of the way we can concentrate on a few necessary skills. I'm going to ask Charles to assist in this part of your training.

As I'd indicated, Charles was a pilot. He grinned. "I get to teach these penguins how to fly?"

"Penguins?" Mac asked with a frown.

"You know, flightless birds. It's a flying joke."

"To be sure. Thank you for enlightening me." I don't think it was sarcasm. Mac had a thing about language. He was always correct and precise in his wording and seemed to enjoy a nicely turned phrase. "No, they already know all they need to know about flying - how to get in an airplane. I want you to help teach them how to stop flying."

Charles' grin got bigger if that was possible. "You mean parachute training?"

"Precisely."

"Damn!" I started to look around before realizing I had spoken aloud. There were a couple titters, but the rest were silent - and just a little scared, too. At least I wouldn't be alone, although I was most likely to be the most scared.

"Come on, Eric," Charles taunted. "Parachuting is as easy as falling out of a plane." He was getting a kick out of this.

"Another flying joke no doubt," I said wryly. "Okay, I'm game - but you get to wash out my pants."

"Are we quite through?" interjected Mac. "We've got a lot of preliminary work if we're going to get in a drop before nightfall. You've got ten minutes to finish your breakfast; then we'll meet at the hangar." He turned around and left.

It's a funny thing. I was scared, as usual, when we went up in the plane. I almost didn't make it out the door. I was hanging there and my hands refused to let go of the sides of the doorway until Vance put his shoe on my behind and pushed me out. It's a good thing we were hooked up to whatever it was called that made sure our 'chutes opened automatically. I was too scared to pull the cord myself. I almost screamed as I shot out of the plane but, fortunately, restrained myself - I'd never have lived it down.

Then there was a sharp tug upward and I was floating gently and silently with most of my classmates strung out in the direction from which we'd flown. My nerves immediately settled down and I was no longer scared. Being supported from above and in the open air, I didn't get the feeling of vertigo you get when you look down a mountain cliff or a tall building - or, for me, an airplane. It was actually quite pleasant, especially since I could see a nice open field below me. Charles had explained that England was an excellent climate for jumping - that was the technical name - because it had nice, thick, moist air which gave us so much support it usually wasn't necessary to land and roll the way we'd just been taught to do.

Mac had interrupted him at that point. "Let's not get too advanced, Charles. You will land the way you were taught. I don't want any broken legs today. Once you've got the experience to judge for yourselves, you can land any way you want to. For now, do it my way."

Charles was right. I had a slight moment of panic as the ground came up to meet me, and I flexed my knees and rolled in the direction I'd been going, as we had practiced, but it really wasn't necessary. I hardly felt the jolt and had so little momentum I didn't really roll, just kind of fell over, feeling slightly foolish. There was just enough breeze that the parachute carried nicely over me and settled to the ground. I understand that, on a completely calm day, you've got to keep rolling to get out from under the 'chute, but it never happened to me.

I gathered up the parachute and stuffed it into its pack - we'd learn to pack it properly the next day, we'd been told - and sat down waiting to be picked up. I was inordinately pleased with myself.

Two days later we started practicing in rougher terrain and we all were a little scared - but that was a justifiable fear, more of a respect for danger. That I could handle. Any dangerous sport requires that kind of respect or you get hurt. While I found I could handle jumping, I still was scared up to the moment the 'chute opened. Then I was all right. Like I said - funny.

Chapter 10

After the first two weeks, we spent the next three months in a combination training and working role. Every once in a while, one of us would disappear for anywhere from a couple of days to a couple of weeks and then return with a grim, but satisfied look. No one was allowed to discuss his mission or even indicate whether or not it was a success.

In the meantime we were kept busy. We studied maps of France and Germany, both flat and topological, as well as aerial photos, until we knew the geography as well as, or better than, that of the U.S. We practiced our languages, practiced surveillance techniques on each other, both in London and in the country, and practiced stalking targets.

The last part was fun, but messy. We were issued air guns, powered by carbon dioxide cartridges, which shot a rubber cylinder filled with dye. The object was to track your victim and get close enough to shoot him without getting shot yourself. To my satisfaction, I had the highest score - on both sides. I averaged over a ninety-percent hit rate when I was the hunter and over sixty percent when I was the victim, even when the instructors started taking part and placing bets.

We also spent a lot of time working with various partners and teams in group efforts. When the exercise required two people, I found that Daryl and I worked the best together. Apparently Mac thought so too, because one morning we were both assigned a mission, the first time two of us had gone on the same mission.

Fedder and Rasmussen woke us and drove us into London, stopping in a blind alley off a side street, next to a dilapidated, gray six-story building. We went in a side door and took a rickety, self-service elevator to the fourth floor - actually the fifth, by our reckoning. The British, in European tradition, start counting floors one floor up. The bottom floor is called the ground floor and the next one up is the first. I guess it makes as much sense as ours does, but it's confusing if the floors aren't clearly marked. The first time I used the stairs in one of their buildings, on a training exercise, the landing numbers had worn off and I counted as I went, ending up one floor too high.

The resulting delay allowed Karl to catch up with me and, instead of being ready for him in my assigned location, he got me in the back before I even got in the door. With typical American arrogance, I cursed the illogical British numbering system and, being upset, went on to make a few choice comments about driving on the wrong side of the street, a money system that was incomprehensible and the general lunacy of measuring things in kilometers, kilograms and liters. I was expanding the tirade to include the inconsistencies in the language when Karl wearily told me to shut up and pointed out that I had a lot of nerve, criticizing a culture that was based on traditions that were old before America, as a sovereign nation, even existed. Didn't I ever consider that it was America that was out of step with the rest of the world, insisting on being different, just out of contrariness? It was a lesson in tolerance that I never forgot and it gave me a new respect for Karl - once I cooled down, of course.

Mac was sitting behind a wooden desk that, while neat, had seen better days. Behind him was a large window affording us a glimpse of a couple of bombed-out buildings. It was hard to see his expression due to the glare from the window, which, I guess, was the idea. One of the reasons we were all so loyal to Mac was his personal touch. If at all possible, he never sent any of us on a mission without doing so face-to-face. He once told me that if he was going to send a man out to die, the least he could do was look him in the eyes when he gave the orders. That was later on, and on this occasion, I was just flattered that the top man himself was doing the briefing. I assumed Daryl felt the same way, not that it was the type of thing one talked about.

Mac explained what we were expected to do. "We have discovered, never mind how, that a certain German gentleman is going to be at a certain place in France in three days. The powers that be would like very much to talk to this gentleman. Furthermore, they would prefer that the German High Command did not know about this particular talk, as they might be of a mind to change their plans should they discover that the plans were compromised."

I won't vouch for the exact words, but it was a fairly typical briefing: we were to do something specific for vague reasons, relying upon intelligence from an unnamed source and, usually, never knowing just how significant the mission was. Hell, half the time I never knew whom I was shooting; someone would point a finger and I'd pull the trigger.

Mac went on. "Rasmussen is in charge. The French underground will get you where you need to go and provide a means of escape, afterwards. You are to not only capture the gentleman in question, but to leave a body in his place, dressed in his clothes complete with his papers to ensure proper identification. Once you are clear, Fedder will blow up the building to, shall we say, hinder a more positive identification of the body. I am assured that a suitable body will be provided by our French friends. Any questions?"

He always ended a briefing by asking if we had any questions. This time someone did. Rasmussen asked, "How will we identify this gentleman?"

"He is a *Luftwaffe* General. The uniform is quite distinctive, and we are told this is an unofficial visit, to be delicate. It is unlikely there will be any other high-ranking officers present to confuse the issue."

We got the message.

Two days later, having survived a night jump with no broken limbs, and being met on schedule, we were lying on a slight rise overlooking a small chalet surrounded by light woods. The trees were heavier in the location Rasmussen had chosen for our initial reconnaissance. Apparently, the General believed in security as there were two German soldiers standing guard outside the otherwise empty building, which made Fedder's job a little more difficult. Fortunately, the Germans didn't feel obliged to patrol the area, being content to sit on the steps leading up to the front door. We had taken the long way around in order to get a view of each side of the building before settling down to let Fedder do his part of the job.

He was good. I never heard him leave and never caught a glimpse of him until he returned two hours later. He nodded at Rasmussen and we left.

We spent the next day planning our strategy, storing up on our sleep and taking turns watching the chalet, just in case the General showed up sooner than expected. Rasmussen drew a perfect diagram of the house and grounds, even to the number and placement of the trees, from memory. I was impressed with his memory as well as his artistry - my attempts at drawing were limited to boxes and "X's", while his could have passed for a blueprint. The final details, of course, had to wait until we saw how many people the General brought with him.

The Frenchman - Jacques was the name he gave us - looked on in boredom. With his lousy English and our lousy French, he didn't waste much time in conversation. Late in the afternoon, two of his associates appeared, carrying what was obviously a body, wrapped in a large sheet of burlap - at least it looked like what I used to call burlap. They nodded at us, accepted a cup of wine from Jacques, and left without a word. I assumed they had come at least part of the way by car or truck, but the road was far enough away we wouldn't have heard it. We unwrapped the body and I got my first look at a dead man, outside of a funeral. We had to look, of course, if for no other reason than to see for ourselves what our General would look like, in a general sort of way, of course - no pun intended. This body was supposed to bear a resemblance to the General if our plan - well, Mac's, to be precise - was to work. I could sense Rasmussen and Fedder watching as I looked down at the body - Daryl had seen one before, having made a couple of them that way himself. He just looked like he was sleeping until we turned him over.

The damage was spectacular. His face wasn't there any more, having been bashed in with something heavy. I would have guessed a baseball bat, if they had any such thing over here. After gulping a couple times, I managed to hold my lunch down, hoping it wasn't too obvious. After a minute, I turned away and saw Fedder looking at me with a mixture of sympathy and approval, which made me feel a little better. Nobody said anything as I walked over and took a drink from the canteen.

At first I was surprised at the method of assassination - there'd been no other wounds on the body - but then it hit me, and I had to admire their professionalism. Jacques - or at least his companions - knew what we were going to do and had carefully obliterated the one thing that could have given the masquerade away, the face. After all, no matter what the force of the explosion, it wasn't guaranteed to hit any victim in any particular part of the body. This way was sure.

Shortly before sundown, having dined on standard Army rations, we were in place on the hill, along with the aforementioned body. Naturally, Daryl and I got that job. In the Army - or any other organization, for that matter - it's called "RHIP." If you don't know what that means, just ask any soldier.

Just as the last light was fading, the General's car drove up and four people got out, including the driver, an enlisted man. The General was easy to spot, and the body was a very good match. The other two were junior officers, also from the *Luftwaffe*, judging from the uniforms. The three of them went into the house, leaving the driver to carry their bags and a couple cartons after them. After three trips, the driver came out and joined the two guards, carrying whatever passed as dinner. The three of them ate as someone inside turned on some music - a light waltz, if it matters. We were glad to hear the music as it would cover any sounds we made outside, if all went well.

We settled down for a short wait, wanting them to get comfortable before we moved. After a whispered conference, we decided upon a plan of attack, which was immediately revised when the driver got up and climbed into the back of the car, presumably to sleep. That complicated matters a little, but Rasmussen told Daryl and me to take the guards, while he and Fedder took the driver. We normally might have waited for the ones inside to go to sleep, but we were expecting one or more women in the party, based on Mac's comment. When the General had arrived without female companionship, Rasmussen had decided to go early while we had fewer people to worry about, just in case the women were due later on. I remembered his remarks about playing the odds, during the training class. He was gambling that the women, if there were any women, wouldn't arrive in the middle of our attack, weighing that possibility against the admittedly harder job if we had more people to deal with, even if the extras were women with supposedly non-violent talents. I'd prefer it if everyone was asleep when I went in the door, but was just as happy not to have to kill a couple of innocent - well, from a combatant standpoint - women. I don't know if that was part of his decision or not, but I was still new to the business. For me, that would have been the deciding factor.

As it turned out, it wasn't a factor. No women were included in the General's plans, for that night, at least.

With the two guards sitting on the steps, there was no way we could get sneak up on them before they raised an alarm. We had to get them with silenced pistols and hope they didn't scream as they were hit. For this purpose, Daryl had been issued a .22 Colt Woodsman identical to mine - I'd kept the one I'd admired during my initial training with Vance. The speed of sound is 1,088 feet per second. It was discovered a while back that for maximum accuracy an ordinary .22 bullet must not be driven faster than that. So farm kids shoot rabbits and squirrels with .22 caliber projectiles that scream along at around 1,200 feet per second, but expert small-bore target shooters settle for something like 1,050. This has another advantage of more importance than championship accuracy to the sinister folk in our line of work. A silencer can muffle the noise of the powder exploding inside the gun, but it can't do anything about the crack of the bullet, outside the gun, passing through the sound barrier. Keeping the bullet velocity subsonic is, therefore, essential to silencing a gun effectively.

Daryl and I slowly crawled forward, keeping behind the trees, until we were less than fifty feet from the house, right at the tree line. We aimed our pistols at the guards, me taking the one on the left - my left, not theirs - since I was to the left of Daryl, and waited until Rasmussen and Fedder had circled around to the side of the building closest to the car. One of them waved in the light spilling out of the window and Daryl and I shot the guards several times each. I doubt if even the guards could have heard the faint puffs from the silenced pistols. For a moment I wondered what had gone wrong as they just sat there; then, as in slow motion, one toppled forward onto the lawn while the other just kind of slumped over against the handrail.

We watched Fedder and Rasmussen come around the corner, each taking one side of the car. Both doors opened simultaneously and I saw the flash of a knife. The guard had been lying with his feet toward the door on our side and we could see his legs do a little jig for a second or two and then he was still.

Up to that point, it had been a perfect operation. The next step had depended upon whether or not there was a warning from outside. Since there hadn't been, the plan called for Daryl and I, who were the closest in size to the guards - they were a Mutt and Jeff team like us - to go in the front door, dressed in their clothes, and Rasmussen to go in the back, while Fedder stood guard until when we came out, or went in after us if we didn't.

While we dragged the guards away from the house and put on their clothes and helmets, disregarding the little bit of blood on them, Rasmussen kept guard. Once we were ready, he whispered, "Count to twenty and then go in," and headed for the back of the house. We walked to the front door, counting, and on twenty, opened the door and walked in.

The idea was, of course, to make them hesitate when they first saw us, giving us time to take care of the two lieutenants while

Rasmussen subdued the General. It should have worked, and might have, if anybody had been in the room. The music was still playing and there were wine glasses on the coffee table, but the room was empty. We looked around quickly. The kitchen was in the back, which was where Rasmussen had come in and it was empty as well. That only left the two bedrooms, one on each side of the living room, both with the doors closed. Rasmussen nodded us toward the one on the right and he headed for the other one.

They were in the one he'd assigned to us. Daryl went in first, being the shorter, so I could shoot over him if necessary. I slammed the door open while he dove inside, rolling quickly to his feet and turning the wrong way. I came in standing - their attention should have been on him, according to our training - and looked the right way. I had the pistol pointed in front of me and turned my head quickly to the right when I found nothing in that direction. The bed was on that side of the room and was occupied...

I might have used the excuse that I was young and naive. Maybe so, but I hope I never get that old and jaded. It shocked me, which is no excuse - after all I had a job to do and had been trained to do that job. Both men were naked, one lying on his stomach, while the other crouched over his legs, doing something obscene with a pistol.

The one with the pistol saw me at the same time I saw him and swung it toward me while I stood there frozen like a gaping idiot, with my own pistol out of position. By the time I could move it was too late. I was dead. I could see his finger tightening on the trigger just as someone yelled my name and something hit me in the side, knocking me out of the way. I heard two shots, so close together they almost sounded as one, and I saw a small hole appear in the forehead of the man with the gun. By now I was fully awake and dove toward the other one. We had been told to leave as few bullet holes as possible on the inside - the outside didn't matter - and I was finally following orders.

I hit him and broke his neck. I'll have to admit that it surprised me almost as much as it did him. I'd known from training that it could be done that way, but I hadn't had any really good reason to think I could do it. I'd been ready to throw myself on top of him and pin him down and finish him off, one way or another, before he could recover from the first blow. It wasn't necessary. There were some ugly, convulsive jerks and twitches as the final, fading signals filtered through the damaged circuits; then he lay limp and still.

By then Rasmussen had come in and we both headed toward the bathroom. The General was no problem. He was crouched in the shower, crying in terror, as naked as his two friends. I went back to see about Daryl, who we'd left standing in the room. He was sitting on the bottom of the bed, holding his left shoulder. With a little grunting, we managed to get the German's jacket off him, baring his shoulder. He had a deep furrow in the fleshy part of his upper arm, just below the shoulder blade. While Rasmussen went to get Fedder and a first aid kit, I took Daryl into the bathroom and cleaned the wound out, holding a towel on it until Fedder came in and bandaged it.

I looked at Daryl and held out my hand. "Thanks, amigo," I said.

He took it, smiled and replied, "Nada."

Chapter 11

Fedder blew the house on schedule and we got away clean. Jacques and his friends got us all to the coast without incident and the Navy got us back to England, where the General was turned over to British Intelligence. I didn't think they would have any trouble getting him to talk, not after seeing him in the bathroom. I carefully suppressed the thought that the perverted bastard deserved it.

For the most part, we were ignored by the M-5 or M-6 guys - whatever the hell they called themselves - and were happy to see Abraham waiting to pick us up, not that I was looking forward to reporting to Mac for debriefing. It had been an amateur performance on my part, even though the others told me to forget it.

Mac surprised me. After listening to Rasmussen's report - which included my momentary lapse - he turned to me in front of the others and said, "The job got done, and very well, Eric. No one expects you to be a machine. You've learned a very valuable lesson and, under the circumstances, a relatively cheap one. It seems you recovered nicely and completed the job just the way you should have."

That made me feel a lot better until he turned to Daryl. "Daryl, on the other hand, seems to be suffering from tender, brotherly feelings for his fellow man. From what I understand, you had a nice clear shot at your target and, instead of taking that shot, decided to push Eric out of the way so you could then shoot while moving, getting shot yourself in the process. If you'd taken that first shot, possibly neither of you would have been shot. On the other hand, it was quite possible that you might have missed when you finally did shoot, and both you and Eric could have been killed. Do you need a refresher course in Rule One, Daryl?"

He had discipline. He flushed slightly, but managed to say, "No, sir," with a steady voice.

"Very well. Perhaps more than one lesson was learned this time. Daryl, report to the infirmary to have that wound looked at by a doctor. The rest of you can report back to base. Congratulations to all of you on an exceptional job." His glance obviously included Daryl and me. That's my kind of boss. Chew you out when you need it, and then forget it.

Outside the building, I burst out laughing at the incongruity of it, joined by Rasmussen and Fedder. "What's so damned funny," Daryl demanded, still smarting.

"I froze, forcing you to save my life, and got you shot in the process," I gasped, " and you ... you ..." I paused for a breath. "You get reamed out for it!"

His lips twitched as he saw the funny side of it, then he was laughing as loudly as the rest of us. I imagine part of it was simply the release of tension at the end of a mission. We stopped by the infirmary and waited while Daryl's shoulder was properly sterilized and re-bandaged. Then we drove back to the camp and got drunk, along with the rest of the group. After all, Daryl was our first casualty.

Two weeks later, Stella went out and didn't come back. Mac broke the news to us one night in the canteen. Even then, he didn't provide us with details, except for one. "I thought you'd all like to know - she did her job and made the touch. She just ran into some bad luck trying to get clear."

That night we all had a drink to Stella's memory. Nobody got drunk.

During the following year, the air war intensified, and our services were requested in the rescue of important prisoners - important in the sense of the information in their heads - as well as the capture of Germans with important information in *their* heads. After the success of the mission in which Daryl got injured, British Intelligence considered us their own private little information-retrieval service for a while, until Mac disabused them of the idea. There weren't many instances when someone was a sitting duck as our General had been, and Mac refused to accept suicide missions that had no chance of success. He didn't have so many agents that he was willing to expend one fruitlessly, and apparently his authority came from high enough up that he could make it stick - which didn't make us any more popular with the intelligence outfits.

After all, he explained to us on more than one occasion, we were trained for a specific purpose. We weren't the search and rescue boys, a commando outfit or an intelligence agency. Our unit was created to do the jobs that nobody else wanted - to get our hands dirty face-to-face with a specified enemy. Finding those kinds of people wasn't easy. If you look, there's evidence that, in most modern wars, the average soldier simply shot his gun in the general direction of the enemy and when given a clear shot at an individual, couldn't bring himself to pull the trigger. Most casualties of war came from the long-range weapons, when you couldn't see the face of your opponent. There were always exceptions, of course; otherwise Mac wouldn't have found enough recruits to form his unit.

Actually, I think he accepted some of the early missions - like my first one, where we actually went in and did the whole job - just to give us some on-the-job-training. He didn't trust an outsider to protect his new people until they graduated, so to speak. Regardless of all the training, no one was really considered a graduate until they actually pulled the trigger, figuratively speaking of course - it could be a knife or garrote or your hands.

We lost one of our group that way. His name was Mark and he was a pain in the ass all through training. He was the gung-ho type, with the movie soldier syndrome. You know what I mean. He considered everyone with perfectly legitimate fears, if not a coward, then certainly lacking in the manly attitude. I'll admit I was prejudiced - he was one of the ones who laughed at my reaction to parachute training. He was the first to belittle someone for a bad score and the first to brag on his own good scores - and they were very good. He was a natural at any weapon and hell on wheels at hand-to-hand. There was more than a touch of bully in him and we were all just as happy when he was sent out on his own and not paired with one of us. Vance went along to chaperone and told us about it later.

It wasn't a high-risk operation, as the French underground did all the work. All Mark had to do was lie down on the ground about three hundred yards back and pull a trigger. It was broad daylight and the target was just standing there. Vance was lying beside him, ready to make sure if Mark missed. The first time you have a real person in your sights instead of a paper target, its easy to get a little excited and rush the shot or shake just enough to pull the bullet off course, which is why we always had company on our first missions. Anyway, Vance waited almost too long, giving Mark the benefit of the doubt. Then, he heard a choking sound and saw the barrel of Mark's rifle tilt down. Looking over at him, Vance saw that Mark was crying. He simply couldn't pull the trigger. He wasn't a coward - he was later awarded a Silver Star for bravery under fire, once he was reassigned to a combat unit where his talents were more appreciated - he just couldn't kill someone in cold blood, something no tests, interviews or training can determine.

Mark, of course, never came back to our base. His things were collected and forwarded to the appropriate unit. Most of us, including Vance, didn't fault him, and those who hadn't yet had the chance to prove themselves were very quiet for a few days. It happens. Fortunately, Vance was able to make the touch and nobody died because of a failed mission.

Ironically, a lot of our missions were like Mark's, especially while we mostly operated in France. Mac was willing to lend a hand when a back-up man who was handy with weapons was needed, so long as the primary risk was taken by others. I spent a lot of time totally removed from the action, waiting for my target to appear, pulling a trigger, and quietly disappearing while all hell broke loose below me. Most of the time I had no idea why I was pulling the trigger or even whom I was shooting. We weren't exactly inundated with information, if you know what I mean.

Chapter 12

Our little group would expand and contract as the war went on, new recruits added and experienced agents dying or being captured - a grim reminder that even a safety zone of three or four hundred yards often wasn't enough. And then there were the times when the long rifles wouldn't get the job done and we had to go in and get them up close.

It was on one of those missions that I got shot the first time. The nice open targets were getting scarce. You can always overdo a thing and it doesn't take large numbers to make an impact. If a doctor discovers five patients in one town who die of arsenic poisoning, it's a pretty good bet that a source of contamination exists. If the same type of engine falls off the same type aircraft three times in 200 sorties, you ground the planes until the manufacturing defect is fixed. Likewise, if a few high-ranking officers in critical positions inexplicably fall down dead just at the wrong - or right, depending on your viewpoint - moment, you start issuing orders to stay out of well-lit windows and don't take walks in the open.

I don't really think the Germans suspected the existence of a group like ours that early on - it was probably put down to the copycat theory. A good idea is a good idea, no matter who originated it. Actually, as Mac observed when he told us of the orders, it probably hindered the German efforts in France as much, or more, than the actions which necessitated the orders. As he put it, a little paranoia was good for their nerves - good for our side, of course.

It did make our job more difficult, so our tactics changed to fit the new circumstances. Ironically, it was another partnership mission with Daryl, another General who was the target, and another blunder on my part, which got me shot. Well, bad luck had a lot to do with it. And good luck allowed me to survive it, so it evens out.

We had infiltrated a small town just outside Paris, a favorite place for German Generals to spend a few days on vacation. We were hidden for two days in a small French café that served bad enough food that the Germans avoided it - letting the Resistance use it for a meeting place. When we got word that our target had arrived and which chalet he had selected for his stay, we moved in.

The plan was to hide in his chalet - the Germans had almost no security at that time, being arrogantly sure that they were safe that close to Paris - and take him as he came in, drunk and with a female companion in tow. A pretty young French girl - so we were informed - with Resistance sympathies had been selected for the purpose. She was to flirt with him, get him drunk and get herself invited to his chalet.

I don't know what went wrong - maybe the girl wasn't pretty enough, or maybe he just ran into some old friends and put friendship above sex for that night. In any case, the door opened and he came in and saw me standing there with a gun, which was part of the plan. I was the distraction. He was supposed to see me and, while his attention was diverted, Daryl would step out from behind the door and slit his throat. That's often why partnerships are used, that and the fact that the partner creating the diversion is available for backup, if needed. The plan worked perfectly up to that point and Daryl performed on schedule. However, as the General fell, his two friends, who had also seen me, burst through the doorway, struggling to get their pistols up to fire - at me, of course. Daryl was hidden from their view by the door and all they saw was the General being jerked backwards. I was the one with the gun, the natural target. They were fairly slow getting their pistols into play - it's not easy getting a gun out of those leather holsters they wear - and I already had mine pointed at them, but I hesitated just long enough for one of them to get off a shot before I killed him. I felt a hammer blow in my chest, but the other one was bringing his pistol up, so I shot him in the head. Then I looked down and saw the round hole in my shirt, with a little blood around it…

Okay, so it was stupid, but if you're a man with a gun who's had any training at all, you don't take any hasty shots toward your partner's position. You get the permissible sectors of fire clearly set in your mind first thing; you remind yourself firmly that shooting in *that* direction is simply not allowed. Just as the AA guns on a warship are blocked so that the ones aft can't blow the heads off the guys serving the ones forward if somebody gets excited, so each member of a good hunting partnership, whatever the quarry, establishes certain limits for himself beyond which he *must* not fire, at least not without thinking it over and being very, very careful. The problem is that when you really *need* to fire in that direction, the warning signals scream in your brain - *danger bearing, danger bearing* - like klaxons going off in there and red lights flashing, make you take a moment to think it over and wait for a safer shot - which may be too late. That's one of the reasons I prefer a lone-wolf operation - I may not have someone watching my back, but at least I don't have to worry about whom I shoot.

Daryl looked at me and asked, "Are you all right?"

Well I was still standing, if a little in shock, so he hadn't hit my heart. And if I had internal bleeding, I figured I might as well bleed to death in a safe place, which this wasn't going to be in a few seconds, so I nodded. "So far, at least. Let's get out of here."

We were lucky, as no one - at least no one who'd talk to the Germans - saw us as we made our way back to the café. Daryl had to help hold me up the last few steps, as I was beginning to feel weak from the pain. It's funny how a bullet always hurts more five minutes later than when it first goes in. Adrenaline, I guess.

I was lucky enough that nothing important had been damaged and there was not much internal bleeding, so with a little disinfectant and a bandage, I stayed alive long enough for a doctor back in London to remove the bullet and patch me up. There wasn't even any infection to worry about, just some bruised feelings - I got essentially the same lecture from Mac that Daryl had received on our first mission together. Well, he might be a bastard, but at least he was a consistent bastard.

Mac didn't put much stock in physical condition. He believed a man's mental condition is what counts and his policy was to get a man back into action as soon as possible and not let him spend too much time pondering his wounds. Two weeks later he sent me back across the Channel with Vance. I had a half-healed bullet hole in my chest, and Vance had his arm in a sling. Mac figured it made our impersonations of German soldiers on convalescent leave much more convincing, and there's no evidence that it affected our performances adversely.

Chapter 13

In the early part of 1944, about six months after I took that first bullet in the chest, I was sitting in Mac's office listening to the most godawful, beat-around-the-bush briefing I had ever heard from Mac. Normally, he was not one to waste words explaining a mission. I mean, the facts of life had been pretty well taken for granted by then, especially among us senior agents - anyone who had survived the first year working for Mac was, by definition, a senior agent. After the first few months I pretty much ran my own shows and, although I had been in charge of two team efforts, I was mostly used in a lone-wolf capacity.

Of the original nine members of my training class, only three were still on active duty with us. Stella had been the first to die, of course, and Mark was the only one of us that never "graduated." However, in late 1943 we lost both Gene and Derek on a botched joint mission. They managed to get into position and make the touch, but the reinforcements didn't arrive. British intelligence had set up a rescue mission in conjunction with the French Resistance. One of BI's people had been taken prisoner and they wanted him back - he supposedly had some vital information our side needed, but had been foolish enough to be captured alive. Our part of the mission was to take out the two guards on the roof of the building in which the British agent was being held and, when the assault force attacked on that signal, provide back-up firepower.

The reason I knew so much about that particular mission was that I had originally been scheduled to go with them, but had been pulled off when something else came up requiring my specialized talents. We found out later that the mission had been canceled by the field commander, due to the arrival of some unexpected reinforcements at the building. The messenger dispatched to inform Gene and Derek of the change in plans was just late enough to witness the debacle. While our two people waited for the nonexistent assault to begin, a machine gun crew, which wasn't even supposed to be there, located their position and got them both. It seemed that my luck was still holding - I could have been there with them

Just over a month later, we lost Charles due to just plain bad luck. He and Nick were jumping into France when his 'chute got tangled in a tree. Before Nick could reach him to help, a German patrol spotted him and a quick burst from a machine pistol negated the necessity for any help on Nick's part. Some of us might have looked unkindly on the German target practice - a man tangled in a parachute some twenty feet up in a tree can hardly be considered a threat to anyone - but Nick took his missions seriously and wouldn't jeopardize one for the sake of a revenge that probably would have just got him killed. Nick was as close to the ideal of a cold, killing machine that I'd ever met. I'm not criticizing - as I've indicated previously, I kind of envied him his lack of emotional involvement in his work. All in all, he was a better man at the job than I, but I really wouldn't have traded places with him.

As a matter of fact, Nick was our last casualty, exact status unknown. In January of 1944, he was sent on an infiltration mission. He was one of the best I'd ever seen at playing the part of a German soldier. He looked like one of Hitler's poster boys, tall, blond and Aryan, with blue eyes and masculine chiseled features. No one could be suspicious of such a fine-looking German boy. He was supposed to bide his time until he could make the touch look like an accident - there are several ways to do this, including a new kind of drug which caused a heart attack and couldn't be detected in the body unless an autopsy was conducted within hours. We never did find out what happened; our informant simply reported seven bodies being carried out of a Nazi headquarters building, one of them a Nazi staff officer who had been Nick's target. I don't know if Nick had made a mistake and simply took as many with him as he could or if he cracked and went on a suicidal rampage. Actually, we just assumed it was Nick - neither his presence nor death was ever confirmed.

If you're wondering why I knew so much about some missions and virtually nothing about others, it had to do with Mac's personal policy. On a successful mission - or even an unsuccessful one, if the agent survived - he respected the security enforced by the "need-to-know boys in charge of war-time intelligence. However, when one of us died or was captured, he made a point of explaining why, within reasonable guidelines. He felt that, when one of us paid the ultimate price, the rest of us had a right to know that the effort was not in vain. And he never sent a spokesman, he told us himself, whoever was in base at the time. It somehow made it easier, the next time we went on a mission, to know that Mac cared about each one of us.

My attention had wandered during Mac's hemming and hawing around the subject, and I realized he had asked a question. Something about would I accept a mission for reasons of vital importance to Allied security, even if the target was innocent.

"Sir," I replied in exasperation, "with all due respect, what kind of pussy-footing bullshit is this!" This was as close as I'd come to insubordination, not to mention profanity - Mac seldom used any profanity, other than an occasional "damn" or "hell", and we were normally careful to avoid it in his presence - and I don't know who was the most surprised, him or me. I braced myself for the expected rebuke, but, after looking slightly startled for a moment, he actually seemed somewhat embarrassed. That's when I knew it was serious.

Without waiting for his reply, keeping my voice steady, I said, "Perhaps you better tell me about it, Sir."

"You're right, Eric, I should have known better ... but this is the first such request we've had."

He paused for a brief moment and then began, sounding more like his normal self. "Last week a gentleman we will call Sir Robert was abducted from his country home outside London. Sir Robert's actual rank and position in the Allied Command structure have not been disclosed to me. Nor has anyone specified the exact nature of the information he has in his possession, I assume in his head. I am, however, informed that said information is not only vital to our prosecution of the war effort, but potentially disastrous to that effort if it falls into the wrong hands. So much so that British Intelligence has compromised several of their intelligence networks and agents in France in a desperate attempt to locate Sir Robert.

"In this they succeeded, although not without cost. Apparently several good men and women have already died, getting this information out without the usual precautions. Fortunately, no one was captured alive, so the Germans are not aware that we have located Sir Robert. After the fact, British Intelligence discovered that Sir Robert was a specified target, ordered by Berlin, and is scheduled to be transported to Berlin for interrogation. Apparently, the information Sir Robert possesses is of such importance that someone high in the German Command wants to take personal credit for obtaining it, so it is doubtful that any serious attempts at interrogation have taken place."

I thought I had it figured out by now. This was the Volunteer Mission - we always capitalized it in our minds - the one where the odds were so bad that even Mac wouldn't order us to accept it. "How much time do we have to get him out?" I asked. I resisted adding, 'and what are the chances of us getting out?' although I'll admit I thought it.

This time Mac surprised me, more than a little. "Not get him out, Eric. It has been decided that a rescue attempt is impossible. You are to take him out. Sir Robert is your target."

He was watching me closely. I paused for a long minute, thinking it over. Then I asked, "This is for real, Sir? I mean, the information is that important, not just some of their security games?" I was hedging, and he knew it, but he answered anyway.

"From what I was told, and by whom I was told it, I would have to say yes. Also, the efforts that are underway to give us a chance to get to him, would seem to underscore the importance placed upon this mission."

I started to ask him what efforts, but realized that would be more hedging. I had killed Germans, as well as a couple of German-sympathizers, not to mention a few assorted innocent bystanders, in defense of my country and its allies. Could I now, in good conscience, refuse to kill someone who - albeit innocently - threatened that defense? These guys who keep drawing lines never impress me very much. I know a dozen fisherman who'll let a trout fight its heart out against a nylon leader, but who are real proud of themselves because they've never shot anything in their lives. And then there's a man I know who'll shoot any bird that flies - ducks, geese, quail, doves, you name it - but he feels quite moral because he's never killed a big animal like a deer or an elk. And I even know a deer hunter who gets his buck every fall but who'd never dream of going to Africa and murdering a great big elephant just for sport, he thinks that's terrible. They've all got something they won't do, and it makes them feel swell. I've always prided myself on not being hypocritical and drawing arbitrary lines for myself. Was this so much different?

I drew a deep breath and said, "How do I do it and how much time do I have?"

Chapter 14

Four days later I was on a hill just outside the small French town of Falaise, looking down on a magnificent French mansion that was surrounded by the entire German Army - well that was my initial impression. They looked like they were expecting an armed invasion, which confirmed what Mac had told me.

After I'd agreed to do the job, he just continued as though nothing unusual had happened.

"You've got almost a week, at least that's what the weather people are saying. Beyond that, it's anybody's guess, so to be safe let's say four days from now. We've stepped up our flight operations from Falaise, where Sir Robert is being held, to Paris to emphasize our search for him. The Germans know how badly we want him, due to the continuing inquiries being sent down the line by British Intelligence, as a cover. We're pretty sure they have no idea we've located him and are just waiting for the next storm front to come in before they move him.

"As to how, it's got to be a long-range rifle job, over four hundred yards, I've been told. I've already got the rifle and the necessary materials for you to hand-load the cartridges and you'll have three days to get the feel of it. We'll drop you Tuesday night. You'll be met and escorted to the area. Try to make the touch during the day Wednesday, saving Thursday for a safety zone."

"Why during the day?"

"Apparently there's a sort of courtyard on the roof of the first floor. We don't know where in the house Sir Robert is being held, but he's allowed out on that courtyard two or three times a day, under guard, of course. That's the only time you'll have a chance at him."

"If they know that much, why don't they just bomb the house."

Mac said wryly, "You seem to have a higher regard for the accuracy of our bombers than our British friends do, Eric. I'm told that a target that small could only be hit for certain, at least on the first try - and we wouldn't get a second - if we sent so many bombers that they would probably guess what's coming and get out before we got there. Even if we hit the house, there is no guarantee that we'd get Sir Robert, and we might never find him again."

"Okay, I guess I'm it. I suppose there's been some thought given to getting me back out? Well, I guess I'll find that out when I get there. Where's the damn rifle?"

"Out at the base, waiting for you at the long-rifle range."

"A little confident, were we?"

"Let's say that I thought you would do the right thing."

I got up and started out the door. He stopped me. "Oh, Eric?"

"Yes, Sir?"

"Thank you. You're the best rifle man I've got."

It was my turn to be a little embarrassed. To cover it I grinned. "De nada, as they say back home."

My contact, to my surprise, was British. His name - well, the name he gave me - was Ryland. As we worked our way to the target area, he told me he was a French citizen, having lived in Falaise for over ten years. He was married to a French girl and ran a small store in the city. He was what they called an "in-place agent." Being British, he was watched by the Germans perhaps a little closer than otherwise, so he was not normally used as anything but a conduit for information being passed down the line. He was more involved in this case because he had to provide a hole for me to crawl into, after completing my mission, until it was safe to move me out of the country. As he put it, Falaise was a quiet little town without many Resistance resources. Besides, he was the one who had found Sir Robert and wanted to see it through to the end.

He recognized my wary look - I'm not exactly thrilled, putting my life in the hands of a noncombatant. There was something about him, but I couldn't quite pin it down.

"It's been a while," he said, "but I've had my share of the - shall we say - more violent pursuits. Not only in the Great War, but a few skirmishes here and there."

Then I placed him. Not that I recognized him, but I knew the type. He was a spare, sinewy man in khakis, very English, with a bushy sandy moustache and sharp blue eyes under sandy brows and lashes. He was about twice my age, but moved younger, if you know what I mean. I looked for the gun, but couldn't see a bulge due to the loose jacket he was wearing. But it would be there, probably the same gun he'd carried for years and put away regretfully when he got married.

Not that a shoulder holster isn't a neat rig for carrying a heavy weapon outdoors in winter; it is. It puts the weight up where it belongs, supported by a substantial harness, instead of down on a narrow belt that tries to cut you in two. You don't have to open your coat much to get at it if you need it, and the gun doesn't freeze up in the coldest weather. A good spring shoulder rig is surprisingly comfortable, the gun is safe even if you stand on your head, it's protected from the elements, and it doesn't get in the way around camp the way a belt gun will. The fact that it's relatively slow needn't worry the outdoorsman, who's not apt, these days, to meet a grizzly on the trail without warning.

That's speaking of a big revolver carried by a hunter or trapper. When it comes to small, flat, inconspicuous automatics packed by competent-looking gentlemen with exaggerated British accents, you're speaking of a different matter entirely. I looked at him grimly. I knew him now. I knew what it was I'd smelled or sensed about him. It was the smell of smoke, of gunsmoke. It never quite blows away. He was a soldier of fortune, one of the armpit-gun boys.

He stood looking at me for a long moment, his face expressionless; and it happened the way it sometimes does regardless of the shade of the skin or the color of the hair or the language spoken by the ancestors. I don't say that we became friends in that instant; but there's a relationship between fighting men that the nonviolent ladies and gentlemen of the world can never understand, which may be why they fear us and pretend to despise us as old-fashioned and obsolete and dreadfully immoral.

Fortunately, the hill on which we were poised was not part of the large estate surrounding the house and was badly overgrown with lots of trees and thick underbrush. We both had some rips and tears in our clothing, not to mention our exposed skin. I couldn't have asked for better cover. We had arrived at dawn and Ryland had led me to the vantage point he had been using to observe Sir Robert's movements. I couldn't see anything wrong with it and told him so. The only thing that concerned me was that the courtyard he pointed out was a lot further away than I'd been led to believe.

I looked at him. "I was told the range would be approximately four hundred yards. About three hundred seventy of your meters. You grow some damn long meters in this country, Ryland."

After making sure I had a clear shot with no obstructions, we backed down out of sight and I reached for the oiled canvas bag containing the rifle. I pulled the long zipper and started pulling out packing material, hoping the heavy bastard hadn't been jarred too much when I landed. We had used an oversized 'chute to minimize the impact and I was able to land on my feet, having missed any trees in the process.

I suppose it was a solemn moment, kind of like finally consummating the marriage after a long courtship. Well, the real consummation was still to come, but I'd spent three full days preparing this equipment and bringing it here; just taking it out

93

should have been celebrated with a little ceremony, say a toast or a prayer. However, it was no time to be drinking, and I've kind of got out of the habit of praying. I just reached in and took the big rifle out of the case, leaving the rest of the packing inside.

It was a heavy match barrel on the long Mauser action, shooting a hand-loaded version of the .300 Holland and Holland Magnum cartridge that I'd cooked up myself. I slipped off the rubber bands and removed the corrugated cardboard that gave additional protection to the scope, a twenty-power Herrlitz. We'd used European components so if we were killed or caught, there wouldn't be too much Yankee debris left lying around. I was carrying my death pill, never mind where, so I couldn't be forced to identify myself as an American. We didn't want anybody wondering why an American citizen was on French soil, murdering an important British officer.

The stock was a plain, straight-grained hunk of walnut without much sex appeal, but it was fitted to the barrel with artistry. A regular G.I. leather sling completed the outfit.

It was quiet there just below the peak of the hill as I got ready, except for an occasional muffled shout from the grounds of the mansion.

I saw Ryland pick up the case I'd dropped, fingering it gently.

"It is an impressive firearm," he said.

"Let us hope the man we came to impress finds it so," I replied.

He glanced at me sharply and started to speak, but checked himself and was silent, watching while I rigged the rifle sling for shooting and dug the box of cartridges out of the bag he held. They were big, fat shells. They looked as if an ordinary service round had had a clandestine affair with some anti-aircraft ammo. I could only get four of them into the gun: three in the magazine and one in the chamber. I stuck the box in my pocket, put the rest of the packing back inside the bag and zipped it up, leaving him to carry it.

With the big rifle in hand, we crawled back to the top of the hill. "Let's see what we've actually got here."

I took the bag from him and folded it for a rest, laying the rifle across it. I had to hunt a bit to pick up my target - those big target scopes have a narrow field - then the soldier standing just below the courtyard was clear and sharp in the glass, but he still wasn't exactly at arm's length. It was going to be one hell of a shot, if I made it.

I lay there telling myself hopefully that at least the wind wasn't blowing. "Five hundred and fifty yards," I said. "Approximately. That, Ryland, is over five hundred of your meters. Your estimate was damn near forty percent off."

"You can read the distance?" He sounded more interested than apologetic.

"There is a scale inside the telescope," I said. "You take a man like that one, approximately six feet tall - at least I hope he wasn't a pygmy or a giant - and you place the lowest division of the scale at his feet and read the range opposite the top of his head, making allowances for the helmet. Then you take this figure and enter the table I have attached to the stock of the rifle, here. You learn that to hit a target five hundred and fifty yards away, the way this particular rifle is sighted at this particular time, you must hold over eighteen inches. In other words, I will have to shoot for the top of the head to hit the chest."

Actually, of course, I hadn't ever believed the story of four hundred yards. I'd sighted the rifle in at four hundred and fifty yards, and run my compensation table from three hundred to six hundred, just in case. There has seldom been a spy yet, or a hunting guide for that matter, who wouldn't underestimate a range badly. You always hope the day will come when somebody will hand you the straight dope, but a forty percent error wasn't much more than par for the course.

"That's what I call progress," Ryland said. I couldn't tell whether he was being ironic or not.

"Sure," I said. "It assumes that I can find a man the right size to take the range from, and that he's standing up straight, and that I'm not looking at him from too great an angle up or down. It assumes the gun it shooting where it was when I made up the table, a few hundred miles away in a different climate. And at five hundred meters, it takes this bullet the better part of a second to reach its target. A walking man can cover six feet in a second, so we'd better hope he stands still for us. What's his routine?"

He grinned at my sarcasm. "You must be very good with that rifle, Eric; otherwise you wouldn't be so pessimistic."

I grinned back. It's nice dealing with professionals. He was right. Only an amateur brags about how good he is with a gun - or any other weapon for that matter.

"Sir Robert is led out by two guards, always," he explained. "They usually stand by the door while he walks around a little. Sooner or later, he will sit down on one of those stools around the table in the middle and have a cigarette or two. Is that still enough for you?"

"Good enough. How long before he comes out?"

"Probably another two or three hours, if he comes out this morning. If not, he'll be out just after noon."

"Okay, you're the spotter," I told him. I'd given him the pair of binoculars I'd brought with me. I want you to be watching through those glasses when I fire. If I miss, you tell me where it goes so I can correct the next shot properly."

"There won't be time for many shots," Ryland said. His expression didn't change, but it was clear nevertheless that he didn't like my talking about misses.

I said, "If there's time for one, there's generally time for two. If I miss, look for the sparks and pieces of concrete where it hits and give me the distance I'm off. In meters or fractions of a meter if you like. Give me the direction by the clock. Twelve o'clock, three o'clock, six o'clock, nine o'clock, or points in between. You understand?"

"Yes. I've shot at the targets, if without much success, at least at this distance."

"Good. Once he's down, try to spot a few extra targets for me until we run out of time. When you say go, we go, okay?"

"Righto, old chap," he replied, grinning. I could find myself liking the guy, if I didn't watch it.

"From what you said, we'll have plenty of warning, so if you don't mind watching by yourself, I'm going to get some sleep. It's been a long three days and an even longer night. Wake me when he first comes out." I slid back down a little, taking the rifle case with me for a pillow. I actually did go to sleep, which I think impressed him more than anything.

About three hours later, he woke me up with a whispered, "Eric!" He knew enough not to touch me. When you wake a professional up by touching him, you risk some fairly unpredictable responses, depending on the circumstances. I yawned and stretched and pulled myself together, splashing some water on my face from the canteen he'd brought with us. I took a swallow and then went behind a tree to take care of some urgent business, no bladder distractions, thank you. I wondered idly how many important shots, and great opportunities, had been missed because somebody had to go at the wrong time.

Picking up the bag, I crawled up beside him and got the rifle into place. I settled myself comfortably behind it and shoved off the safety, double-checking, by looking, that it was really all the way off. That's another mistake that's been made by people who should have known better, including me. Then I remembered the box of cartridges, still in my pocket. Well, nobody's perfect. Now I knew why my thigh was a little sore. I must have rolled over on the box in my sleep. I opened it and set it where I could reach it easily. I didn't know if I'd have time to reload, but Mac had suggested - and I'd explained to Ryland - that it wouldn't hurt to have more than one dead body down there, just to confuse the issue a little - with Sir Robert just one of several victims, a case could be made for him being in the wrong place at the wrong time. We didn't particularly care what the Germans thought, but if rumors of a firefight at the mansion leaked out, the more casualties the better. We should have a fair amount of time, due to the high wall surrounding the grounds, with no opening anywhere near the base of our hill.

Ryland was right. The two guards stood right there by the door, perfect secondary targets, as Sir Robert walked around and back and forth across the courtyard. Then it was just a matter of waiting. I'm not an iron man; I had the usual quota of palpitation and perspiration. I resisted the temptation to look around, perhaps selecting other targets. I also resisted the impulse to try for him during his momentary stops; if he started moving again, the bullet would strike behind him. I just lay there forcing my body to relax along the ground. I was just an eye at the ocular, a finger on the trigger.

After almost ten minutes that seemed like two hours, my mind was beginning to whisper the thoughts you try to keep suppressed: *You could have got him that time, you idiot. Maybe he's given up smoking and never sits down. Look at him standing there looking over the wall, a perfect target.* It comes with the territory. All you can do is grit your teeth and try to think of something else. Fortunately, Ryland knew enough to keep silent, although I could hear the rustling sounds as he stirred from time to time - no doubt he had his own demons.

Finally, Sir Robert sat down in one of the stools and lit a cigarette. He had chosen the one closest to our position, putting his back to us, a nice broad, tempting target. Instead, I settled the crosshairs on the cowlick on the top of his head. I heard Ryland stir impatiently beside me, still silent. I wasn't aware of adding the last fraction of an ounce to the pressure already on the trigger, but the big rifle fired.

It made a hell of a noise in the quiet valley; it was like setting off a cannon-cracker in church. It slammed back against my shoulder and cheek. It's not a fun gun to shoot.

"Call it," I said, working the bolt fast and trying to pick up my target again in that lousy scope. "Call it, damn you!"

"He's hit," Ryland said calmly. "He is falling off the stool."

Then I had my man back in the field. He had slumped across the table and slid off to the deck. I gave it the same rough eighteen inches of Kentucky elevation and fired again. There was the same volcanic eruption and the same piledriver blow against my face and shoulder.

"Good show, old chap," Ryland said in his calm voice. "Here come the guards. "

As I yanked the bolt back and slammed it home again and brought the scope back in line, I could see the two guards bending over Sir Robert. They didn't really know what was going on. The thunderous report of the Magnum would have sounded vague and directionless down there, like distant blasting. At that range you can shoot at a deer all day, if you're that bad a shot, and he'll never even stop browsing until you land one close.

I took out the first guard, but the second one finally got smart and ran for the door. Giving up on him, I chambered the last round as Ryland started spotting additional targets.

"To your left, about ten meters, just below the courtyard. Why aren't they taking cover?"

I didn't waste my time explaining, concentrating on getting as many shots in as I could. Since the target didn't matter, I took the most conspicuous one, an officer just standing there looking around for the source of the distant - to him - sounds he couldn't identify. I settled the crosshairs on the insignia of his hat and let go. I started hand-loading and got two more in three shots before they started scattering. It was confused as hell down there and they still hadn't located our position. I reloaded, feeling a little ashamed at myself for taking advantage of their lack of training for a situation such as this.

I mean, ours was a new type of warfare for them. They were trained to respond to a direct assault or even long-range artillery fire. This kind of sudden death accompanied by a small "pop" wasn't something they were used to. One brave soldier stood behind his machine gun, moving it back and forth in our general direction, hoping to spot a target. I hope they gave him a medal - posthumously, of course.

I think we got lucky. From the total confusion apparent in the scene below, the officer I shot must have been the commander of the detachment, and nobody seemed to be giving any orders. We heard the "rat-a-tat" of machine gun fire, but no bullets came near enough to our position to notice.

I guess the second guard had finally raised the alarm, because several officers came running out of the front door of the mansion. As they paused in astonishment at the sight of their men running around in all directions, I got one more. As I looked around for a second one I heard Ryland's calm voice.

"I say, old boy, that last shot seemed to have done it. They've located us."

I looked around the scope and saw two officers pointing at us - well, in our direction - and screaming orders. With leadership once again established, several soldiers started toward the gate to get to our hill. I sent the last two shots in their general direction to slow them down, then grabbed the rifle bag and started crawling down the backside of the hill, followed by Ryland.

As soon as we could stand without being seen, we took off as rapidly as the underbrush allowed. With the head start we had, as well as knowing the best path through the brambles and bushes, we never even saw any Germans.

After all the planning and the excitement of combat, the escape was anticlimactic. I spent three days hidden beneath the floorboards of a safehouse - a hiding place that was used for the French equivalent of the Civil War's "underground railway" - and then was brought back to England by boat, once the hue and cry had settled down.

Mac congratulated me and gave me a week off in London. The official story was that Sir Robert had bravely committed suicide to avoid interrogation by the *Gestapo*. The Germans might have told a different story, but they weren't asked. I never saw Ryland again, but would have been proud to work with him, anytime, had the occasion presented itself.

Chapter 15

I'm not particularly tolerant, and I don't really believe that everybody's equal. Depending on what I needed him for, I'll judge a man by his IQ, or the score he makes on the target range, or the speed at which he can take a car around a track; and anybody who tries to tell me that some people aren't brighter than others, or better shots, or faster drivers, is wasting his time. But except for recognition purposes, I've never found the color of a man's skin to be much significance in our line of work, and the idea of killing off a bunch of people just because of a slight chromatic difference or religious belief seemed fairly irrational to me.

As more and more information leaked out of the German-occupied territories, the full picture of the systematic genocide on the part of Hitler's regime against the Jews became painfully clear. We began getting requests for action against various concentration-camp officials, apparently on the rationalization that they deserved to die for their atrocities, never mind the military importance of the target. It was like we were a new toy in the hands of the bureaucrats, the ones who knew of our existence, and they wanted to expand the rules of the game.

Mac wasn't playing. "We're not avenging angels," he told us once at our base outside London, "and we're not judges of right and wrong. It would satisfy my soul to sign the death warrant of every concentration-camp official in the Third Reich, for instance, but it wouldn't contribute much towards winning the war. We're not in business to satisfy my soul or anybody else's. Keep that in mind."

There was, of course, one exception to this rule. Whether to satisfy our souls or prosecute the war, we did try for Hitler himself - that is, certain optimists and egotists among us did, on three different occasions. I had no part in that. It was on a voluntary basis, and I'd taken a look at the preliminary reports on the job and come to the conclusion that it couldn't be done, at least not by me.

I wasn't going to get myself killed volunteering for the impossible, although under orders I'll stick my neck out as far as anybody.

After the third attempt - from which, like the first two, no one returned - counter-intelligence started hearing of queries from the continent, reaching the German espionage apparatus in Britain, concerning the possible existence of an Allied *Mordgruppe* aimed at *Der Fuehrer*. This, of course, although a little off the beam, wouldn't do at all. For the Germans to suspect the existence of anything remotely resembling our organization - whether aimed at Hitler or anybody else - was bad enough; what really worried Mac, however, was the possibility of the rumor getting back to the States.

All the Germans could do, aside from taking a few precautions, was squawk; but the outraged moralists back home could put us out of business in short order. Killing Nazis was very commendable, to be sure, but it must be done, they'd cry, according to the rules of civilized warfare: this *Mordgruppe* sort of thing was dreadful, besides being very bad propaganda for our side. I wonder just how many good men and good ideas were sacrificed before the shiny, cellophane-wrapped god of propaganda. There were times when I got the distinct feeling that even winning the damn war was frowned upon because it might have an adverse effect upon our public relations somewhere, perhaps in Germany or Japan.

Anyway, our activities were sharply curtailed for several months, and all further volunteers for the Big One, as we called it, were told to relax and forget it; henceforth we'd confine our attentions to less conspicuous targets. Mac's worst enemies had always been the gentle folks back home. As he'd said himself once, there wasn't much danger of the Nazis breaking us up, but one softhearted U.S. Senator could do it with a few words. Ironically, it seems to be all right to plan on, and create the machines for, exterminating millions of human beings at a crack, but just to send out a guy to rub out another who's getting to be an active menace, that's considered very immoral and reprehensible. I must say that I don't get it. Why honor and respect a guy who drops a great indiscriminate bomb, and recoil in horror from a guy who shoots a small, selective bullet?

I knew a pilot who flew the Flying Fortresses, dumping death and destruction all over Germany. So finally the flak got his plane, and he bailed out. On the ground, he ran into a German soldier. He had his trusty forty-five out, and he probably could have gotten away, but he couldn't bring himself to shoot a man, not face-to-face like that, in spite of all the people he'd helped kill by remote control, so to speak. The German shot him, of course. And he wound up in a prison camp. I visited him in a London hospital where he had been evacuated after being freed in late '44 or early '45. I remember him explaining how he felt when he saw the German, but it was like speaking a foreign language as far as I was concerned. He went home crippled and sick and wasn't much use after that. He could be ruthless as hell saving the world for democracy as long as he was just pushing buttons umpteen-thousand feet up in the sky but couldn't bear to slam a forty-five-caliber slug into a real live human Nazi at point-blank range.

Chapter 16

I never discovered where or from whom Mac got his orders. It was fascinating to try to imagine the scene. I couldn't picture a straight-backed West Point graduate actually putting it into plain English; certainly it was never set down in writing, and you'll find no records of our activities in the archives of the Department of War.

I used to visualize a conference room with a sentry at the door, very hush, with high-ranking general officers in secret conclave and Mac just sitting there in his gray suit, listening.

"There's the fellow von Schmidt," says General One.

"Ah, yes, von Schmidt, the fighter-group man," says General Two. "Based near St. Marie."

"Clever chap," says General Three. This would be in London or somewhere nearby, and they'd all have picked up something of that insidious clipped British way of speaking. "They say he'd have Goering's job if he'd learned how to bend that stiff Prussian neck. And if his personal habits weren't quite so revolting, not that Goering's are anything to cheer about. But I understand that there isn't a female under thirty within a hundred kilometers of St. Marie with a full complement of limbs and faculties who hasn't been favored with the general's attentions - and they're pretty fancy attentions. He's supposed to have a few wrinkles that Krafft-Ebing overlooked."

Mac would shift position in his chair, ever so slightly. Atrocities always bored him. We didn't, he'd say, go around killing people simply because they were sons of bitches; it would be so hard to know where to draw the line. We were soldiers fighting a war in our way, not avenging angels.

"The hell with his sex life," says General One, who seems to be of Mac's persuasion. "I don't give a damn if he rapes every girl in France. He can have the boys, too, for all I care. Just tell me how to get my bombers past him. We take it on the chin every time we come within range of his fields, even with full fighter escort. Whenever we learn how to counter one set of tactics, he's got a new one waiting for us. The man's a genius, professionally speaking. If we're going to be given targets beyond him, I recommend a full-scale strike at his bases first, to knock him out of the air for a long time at least. But I warn you, it's going to come high."

"It would be convenient," says General Two in a dreamy voice, after some discussion of this plan, "if something should happen to General von Schmidt during the attack, or maybe just a little before it. Might save the lives of some of our boys, if he wasn't around to give the last-minute orders; besides keeping him from being back in business within the month."

Nobody looks at Mac. General One moves his mouth as if to get rid of a bad taste. He says, "You're dreaming. Men like that live forever. Anyway, it seems like a sneaky and underhanded thing to wish for, but if he should happen to fall down dead, about four in the morning of April seventeenth would be a good time. Shall we adjourn, gentlemen?"

I don't vouch for the language or the professional terminology. As I say, I never learned how it was really done; and I never was a general or even a West Point graduate; and as far as aviation was concerned, it was all I could do, even during the war, to tell a Spitfire from a Messerschmidt. Planes were just something I climbed into, rode in a while, and then climbed out of after we'd landed on some strange and bumpy field in the dark - or jumped out of with a parachute, which always scared me silly. Given a choice, I always preferred to start a mission with a boat ride. I suppose that is another thing I owe to some ancestral Viking; for a man brought up in the middle of what used to be called the Great American Desert, I turned out to be a pretty good sailor. Unfortunately, a great deal of Europe can't be reached by boat.

The German general's name was actually von Lausche instead of von Schmidt, and he was based near Kronheim instead of St. Marie - if such a place exists - but he was, as I've indicated, a military genius and an 18-carat bastard.

That particular job had taken only a week. We'd made our touch right on schedule, earning a commendation from Mac, who wasn't in the habit of passing them around like business cards - but it had been a tough assignment, and Mac knew it. He gave us a week to rest up in London, afterwards, and we spent it together. We'd managed, quite illegally, to promote a car - a little twenty-seven horsepower Morris - that I was always having to use my Boy Scout knife on and dismantle that ridiculous electric fuel pump they must have got direct from the Tinker-Toy people. She was very impressed with my cleverness as, of course, she was supposed to be. That made a total of two weeks. I hadn't known her previously, and I never saw her again. If anyone asked me to guess, I'd have said she was still over in Europe. She was a fierce, bloodthirsty, shabby little waif with the gauntness of hunger in her face and the brightness of hate in her eyes.

She carried a paratrooper's knife somewhere in her underwear and a capsule of poison taped to the nape of her neck, hidden by her hair. She always held the knife as if she was about to chip ice for a highball; it had been strictly an emergency weapon with her. I still carried the folding knife of Solingen steel that she'd watched me take from a dead man to replace the knife that he'd broken, dying. I remembered the wet woods at Kronheim, and the German officer whose knife was in my pocket, and the way the blade of my own knife had snapped off short as he flung himself convulsively sideways at the thrust. As he opened his mouth to cry out, Tina, a bedraggled fury in her French tart's getup, had grabbed his Schmeisser and smashed it over his head, silencing him but bending the gun to hell and gone.

I'd first made contact with her in a bar, pub, bierstube or bistro - take your choice according to nationality - in the little town of Kronheim, which is French despite its Teutonic-sounding name.

107

To look at her, she was just another of the shabby little female opportunists who were living well as the mistresses of German officers while their countrymen starved. She had a thin young body in a tight satin dress, with thin straight legs in black silk stockings and ridiculously high heels. I had briefly noted the big red mouth, the pale skin and the thin, strong cheekbones, but her most striking feature was her big violet eyes, at first sight dead and dull. Then, those seemingly lifeless eyes had shown me a flash of something fierce and wild and exciting as they caught my signal across the dark and smoky room that was filled with German voices and German laughter, the loud overbearing laughter of the conquerors. It was inconceivable at the time that I would soon be making love to this girl in a ditch in the rain, while uniformed men beat the dripping bushes all around us.

General von Lausche had his quarters - you could spot them by the armed guard in front - only a few doors down the street from the tavern I've already mentioned. I kept a long-range watch over the house after I'd made my contact with Tina. It wasn't in the orders, precisely. In fact, I was supposed to show no interest in the place at all, until the time came. I didn't really know what I was watching for, since I'd already received from Tina a full report on von Lausche's habits and the routine of the guards, but it was the first time I'd worked with a woman, let alone a young and attractive girl who'd deliberately placed herself in such a position, and I had a feeling I'd better keep myself handy.

The feeling paid off later in the week. It was a gray evening, and Kronheim was having a little wet, belated snow just to make things more pleasant. There was a stir of movement and Tina came running into sight partially undressed, a small white figure in my night glasses. She stumbled past the guards out into the slush of the street, carrying in her arms what was apparently the cheap dark skirt and jacket she'd worn into the place an hour earlier.

I hurried out and intercepted her as she came around a nearby corner. I don't know where she was going, and I don't think she knew, either. It was strictly against instructions and common sense for me to contact her so openly and so close to our target; and taking her back to my place was sheer criminal folly, endangering the whole mission as well as the French family sheltering me. But I could see that I had an emergency on my hands and it was time to shoot the works.

Luck was with us - luck and the lousy weather. I got her inside unseen, made sure of the lock on the door and the blind on the window, and lit a candle; it was an attic room, not wired for lights. She was still hugging the bundle of clothes to her breasts. Without speaking she swung around to show me her back. The whip had made a mess of her cheap blouse and underwear, and had drawn considerable blood from the skin beneath.

"I'll kill the pig," she whispered. "I'll kill him!"

"Yes," I said. "On the seventeenth of the month, two days from now, at four in the morning, you'll kill him."

That was what I was there for, to see that she didn't go off half-cocked - it was her first mission with us - to make sure of the touch, and to get her out alive afterwards, if possible. There might be guards to silence; that was also my job. I was kind of a specialist at silencing guards silently. I never touched her, or even indicated that I might like to, those first half-dozen days. After all, I was in charge and it would have been bad for discipline.

"You mean," she whispered, "you mean, you want me to go back?" Her eyes were wide and dark, violet-black now, deep and alive as I'd never seen them. I found myself, quite irrelevantly, wondering just how some middle-level bureaucrat in headquarters had gone about describing the color of Tina's eyes. "Back to that swine?"

I drew a long breath and said, "Hell, kid, you're supposed to enjoy it."

Slowly the darkness died out of her eyes. She sighed, and touched her dry lips with the tip of her tongue. When she spoke again, her voice had changed, becoming flat and toneless: "But of course,

Cheri. You are quite right, as always. I am being stupid, I love to be whipped by the general. Help me on with the clothes, gently."

Two days later, we laid in the bushes while they hunted us in the dark and the rain. I ran my finger lightly over the scabbing gash across the back of her bare arm. "How bad is it," I asked.

"Not so bad now. We killed the pig, didn't we?" she murmured. "We killed him good."

And we killed the one who almost caught us as we were getting away, and, hiding in the bushes, waiting, we made love like animals to wipe out for her the memory of that Nazi beast. And then the planes came in, those beautiful American planes, coming right on the hour, on the minute, coming in with the dawn, filling the sky with thunder and the earth with fire.

Chapter 17

"Good morning, Eric," Mac said. "Did you and Tina enjoy your little vacation?"

I had just said goodbye to Tina and was still feeling the lingering effects of a wartime romance, this time from the opposite viewpoint. I was the one who watched the other go off to war - if you could call what we do war. Tina had been assigned another mission the previous day and had left this morning.

Having given us the opportunity to rest up and recuperate from a difficult mission, I guess he felt I needed to get back to work before I started brooding about her. In a way, it was like having a second mother, working for Mac. Not that he was warm and loving, by any stretch of the imagination, but he felt he knew exactly what was best for us at any given time, just like my mother. The fact that we disagreed with his assessment was entirely beside the point, just like my mother. And the sad part was that, after the fact, he usually turned out to be right, just like my mother. It was funny, in a way, and probably some psychologist would make a big deal of it, but none of us ever compared him to our fathers. He just projected a mother image, albeit a particularly feral, deadly mother.

I tried to shake that thought out of my mind. Sometimes it seems Mac can read my mind - I'd heard others voice the same thought - and I wasn't sure I wanted to be anywhere around if Mac ever got the idea we compared him to our mothers.

"We enjoyed it very much, Sir," I answered his question. "At least until this morning," I added, dryly.

"I only promised you a week, Eric. The war presses on and Tina was needed for a special job. Just like I need you for one." His voice was slightly reproving. He was not one to put up with much complaining, and I had taken one step too far with my last comment.

He went on in his normal voice, having made his point. "It seems you have some professional driving experience." It was not a question.

Before the war, as kids will, I used to play around with some fairly rapid machinery. I raced some and covered other races with a camera; and a couple of times, on assignments for Mac, I had occasion to do a little driving under fairly hectic conditions.

"I don't know that you would call me a professional, Sir, but I did do a little racing."

"That's what I meant. Does your expertise also include starting an automobile when the owner has the keys and is not anxious to share them with you?"

"You mean hot-wiring a car? Yes, I guess you could consider me experienced in that area. I used to hot-wire my Dad's old pick-up when he wasn't around, until he caught me at it one time and started watching the odometer. But I haven't tried it since the time in college when I lost my keys while ..." I shut up, remembering what I *had* been doing when I lost them. Some things were none of his business, damn it!

He continued without comment. "I assume it's not something you forget. I have a team that needs a car expert, and you're as close as we've got."

I didn't say anything to that. If Mac needed a driver, he could find one. Apparently he needed a driver with some extra talents. The nice thing about working for Mac was that he didn't believe in wasting resources. If a job seemed a little demeaning at first, you could bet that, before it was over, you would have brought into play some of the specialized training you'd received to get out alive.

"Everyone will have his own assignment, but in the event of problems, you will be in charge. This will be your first time into Germany itself, however, so I've assigned a new agent, Herman, to help you out. He was born near Loewenstadt and knows the country, so he can help you plan your escape. In France we have much more help available; however, in Germany, getting clear is often the hardest part of the mission. Herman should be of assistance in this area."

"Who else is in the team?" I asked.

"Jacob, Thomas and Brent are the other three. You haven't met them yet. Thomas will make the touch, while the rest of you provide backup and camouflage. Jacob will play the part of a German Colonel, with Brent and Thomas as his assistants. You and Herman will be enlisted, Herman a personal aide and you, of course, the Colonel's driver."

"I assume the car is up to me?"

"That's right. You will steal an appropriate vehicle in or near Loewenstadt and drive it to your destination, which will accomplish three things. It will get you far enough away so the theft will not likely be noticed; it will make the car look suitably driven and dusty; and it will provide you with a - I believe the term is 'get-away car'?"

"Yes, Sir," I agreed. "As in Jimmy Cagney movies."

"I believe that's where I heard the term." As usual, he ignored my feeble attempt at humor.

"What's the destination and who's the target?"

He told me.

Chapter 18

I took us through the city through the sparse evening traffic and sent the overpowered beast snarling up the long grade out of town. There was a release of sorts in turning loose all that horsepower. I've always enjoyed driving, fast or slow, but fast added to the enjoyment. The fact that I was driving in enemy territory with my life on the line in more ways than one, somehow added to the thrill. I do what I do because I'm good at it, which makes me lucky. The world is full of people stuck in jobs that don't suit them. To some extent, it's the danger that drew me to it and kept me in it. I never gamble with money, because neither winning nor losing money means a hell of a lot to me. But when I gamble my life, that's something else again. The biggest goddamn crap game in the world. It's a compulsive thing, and very few women seem to have it. Maybe that makes them more sensible than men, I don't know; but I can tell them they're missing something.

It was a big black Mercedes I'd stolen outside Loewenstadt, with a six-cylinder bomb under the hood, a four-speed transmission as smooth as silk, and a suspension as taut and sure as a stalking tiger. A few miles out of town I let it out a bit. When I glanced at the speedometer - on a dirt road, yet - the needle was flickering past a hundred and eighty kilometers per hour, which translates to a hundred mph and some change. And I'd thought I was kind of babying the heap along.

It almost scared me to death, but for the rest of that job I was known as Hot Rod, and all driving chores that came up were left to me without argument, although I could get an argument from that bunch of prima donnas on just about any other subject.

Well, I never saw any of them again, and some of them hated my guts and I wasn't very fond of theirs, but we moved our sniper into position and made our touch on schedule, so I guess it was a pretty good team while it lasted. Mac didn't believe in letting them last very long. One or two assignments, and then he'd break up the group and shift the men around or send them out to lone-wolf it for a while. Men - even our kind of men - had a perverse habit of getting friendly if they worked together too long; and you couldn't risk jeopardizing an operation because, despite standing orders, some sentimental jerk refused to leave behind another jerk who'd been fool enough to stop a bullet or break a leg.

I remembered solving that little problem the hard way, the one time it came up in a group of mine. After all, nobody's going to hang around in enemy territory to watch over a dead body, no matter how much he liked the guy alive. I'd had to watch my back for the rest of the trip, of course, but I always did that, anyway.

I was hoping to get a chance to try out some of Hitler's new roads, but progress seemed to have passed by this particular part of the country. By the time we arrived at the town Mac had described, never mind the name, we were suitably dusty and travel-worn. We checked into the hotel and found that they had been properly notified of our arrival and had accommodations prepared - four rooms. It seemed the German Army operated similar to our own. Our three officers each rated their own room, while we lowly enlisted types were forced to share one. I made a mental note to ask for an officer role on my next undercover assignment, not that Mac would pay attention to any such request. Assignments were strictly on a mission-requirement basis, and officers were usually too high-profile. You attracted less attention as an enlisted man. Actually, I didn't mind it so much except for sharing accommodations - I like sleeping alone, or at least choosing my own roommates.

After getting settled into the hotel, Herman and I did a quick reconnaissance of the General's home and found the neighboring house Mac had described to me. It had the right vantage point and was located just over a hundred and fifty yards away. Perfect. I had to admit I was impressed with whoever was responsible for the intelligence work on this job. The neighbor was, I was told, a widower who lived alone and was somewhat of a recluse. The only other house in sight was far on the other side of the General's.

It was a nice quiet street and I didn't foresee any problems and we headed back to the hotel to brief the others.

Our primary target was a *Luftwaffe* General who, our intelligence said, was the most likely candidate to replace another General as commander of a top secret German project, so secret we couldn't be trusted with the details. The current commander was scheduled to get sick and die in the very near future, and Allied Command didn't want our particular General to succeed to the post.

As Mac had put it during my briefing, we couldn't add much to the total casualty count of the war, but we could make an impact all out of proportion to our flyweight status. "Wasps, Eric," he had said. "That's what we are. A wasp doesn't weigh very much and doesn't even have that powerful a sting - it may hurt, but it certainly isn't fatal. Most of the time you probably just ignore a wasp. But take a certain set of circumstances, say four big men driving down the highway at a high rate of speed. Let that wasp fly in the window and start darting around. It is possible for that wasp to so distract the attention of the men that the driver loses control of the car, drives off the road and crashes into a tree.

"When the dust has settled, four men are dead, a two-ton vehicle is totally demolished and the wasp flies gently out the window to freedom, leaving behind no evidence whatsoever of the cause of the accident. If one or more of those men are important enough, a major impact on history had been accomplished by an insect weighing a fraction of an ounce."

I had to admit it was an intriguing analogy. Matthew Helm, wasp. Well, I've been called worse things. The main difference was that what we did was not an accident, no matter how distracting it might be to the enemy. It was nice to think what we were doing was that important, but it would have been nicer to know what the hell we were accomplishing most of the time. We had to kill this General, someone else would kill another General, and the result would help the war effort in a way we weren't trusted to know.

From then on it was absurdly easy. That night the General was having a party out on his patio in the spring weather. We pulled up a short distance away from the neighbor's house, approaching from the direction opposite the General's and parked just off the road, hidden from view by the trees. As planned, Jacob and Thomas got out and went to the front door while the rest of us stayed in the car.

Within forty-five minutes we heard the muffled sound of two shots, evenly spaced. As our cover story required, we pulled out on the road and drove to the front of the neighbor's house. Just as we pulled up, there was a third and final shot. Herman and Brent got out and stood guard with two brand-new German MP40s at the ready. The MP40 is not as nicely made a firearm as the MP38 that preceded it, but was much easier and cheaper to manufacture. It's an ugly beast. I've seen handsome rifles and truly lovely shotguns - the British make some real beauties - but I've never seen a good-looking machine pistol, although I'll admit the old Thompson with the drum magazine had a certain brutal charm. But the misshapen little killing machine, the MP40, was a well-tested and reliable piece of equipment.

We waited, keeping an eye on the General's house. No one came out. We could see the back corner of the patio, where several people were forming a knot over what we hoped was the General's body. No one seemed to be looking in our direction, although with the light in their eyes and our car in darkness, it was unlikely they would be able to see us. After sweating it out for what seemed like several minutes, but was probably no more than thirty seconds, Jacob and Thomas came out of the door sans the scoped sniper rifle Thomas had carried inside and the handgun that Jacob had stuffed into his waistband.

Brent opened the back seat door, the signal that we were still clear, and followed them into the back seat while Herman climbed in beside me. It was my call at that point and I decided upon the least exposure, not knowing how much time we had before someone came out. I quickly made a U-turn and headed back the way we had come. As we turned the corner out of sight of the house, Brent confirmed that we were in the clear. Breathing a collective sigh of

117

relief, we headed for the main road out of town, toward France and our rendezvous point, some three days away.

Once we reached the outskirts of the city, to break the silence, I finally asked, "How'd it go?"

I immediately regretted the question. I should have complimented them on a good, clean job - or even better, kept my mouth shut. As I figured, Jacob took offense.

"What do you think?" he retorted. "You think you're the only one who knows his job? It went perfectly. Thomas got the General with his first shot, the second was just insurance, and I took care of the lousy Nazi as planned."

As I've said before, temperament. Jacob had made it obvious he felt he should have been in charge. I might modestly mention here that I had been getting a reputation as Mac's fair-haired boy - no pun intended - who was sent in on the tough ones. My associates being who they were, some resentment was natural. Also, as I mentioned earlier, I had been forced to shoot one of our own on a previous mission just so two idiots didn't get us all killed trying to carry the guy out. The fact that he was dying anyway didn't matter to some of our more tender-hearted members. I'd only heard of one other agent who'd made the same decision since then, and he was right here - good old fanatical Jacob, who wasn't any more popular than I was with the rest of the group.

Well I didn't like Jacob either, but not because he'd killed one of us. When I first met him, back in London in Mac's office, he'd seemed a little intense and arrogant, but that was pretty usual around there. Then he'd turned his head and looked at me; and I changed my mind about him abruptly. He had those nice, clear, blue, Scandinavian eyes; but they didn't really see me. They didn't see anybody. They were fanatic's eyes that saw only a shining cause, a glorious goal in the remote distance towards which this boy was marching; and if he had to kill you and wade through your blood to get there, that was your problem. I don't think I scare more easily than the average guy, but true believers always give

118

me chills, regardless of what they happen to believe in at the moment. There is no reason or mercy, and more important, there is no humor in them.

I guess Mac had to work with whatever material was available and I had to admit that you probably couldn't find a better candidate if you were looking for the killer instinct. However, this guy had a big hate going and viewed all Germans as Nazis. Although his appearance was a little out of the stereotypical movie ideal - he was tall and blonde with Nordic features - I guessed from his code name that he was Jewish. Well, I wasn't any more thrilled than he was about the genocide going on in Germany and Poland, but hating all Germans for the actions of a relatively small group of butchers seemed almost as irrational, to me at least.

I think that's why Mac had sent Jacob along with us. Our plan was, as usual, to try to cover our tracks. Whenever possible, we tried to make our operations seem like random acts, rather than cold-blooded assassinations. We didn't want the Germans to get the idea that we even existed, especially after the rumors resulting from the aborted attempts on Hitler. Actually, the plan was a little more cold-blooded than usual. An innocent neighbor - we never did know his name - was being set up to take the blame. It actually served two purposes, because we couldn't very well leave him behind to provide descriptions.

That, of course, had been the purpose of the third shot. Our experts had somehow obtained a sample of the neighbor's handwriting and other experts had forged a simple suicide note, brief and to the point: "God forgive me. General"(classified) "was a traitor to the German people." I thought that was a nice touch. It might be cause for some investigation of the General's friends and associates - Hitler was notoriously paranoid. Obviously a suicide note required a suicide, so Jacob was assigned the job of shooting the neighbor with the pistol he had brought along for the purpose.

The idea was that the neighbor would be discovered dead by his own hand, both the pistol and the rifle found in his bedroom beside him, and the note tying it up in a pretty package. Any questions

119

concerning how a peaceful citizen - there was no evidence that he was a Nazi, despite Jacob's epithet to the contrary - had obtained a scoped rifle and a military sidearm, not to mention where he had learned to shoot someone - twice - at a hundred and fifty-yard range, would be lost in the shuffle. When dealing with the authorities, try to give them a nice, simple solution to a problem. They'll refuse to let it be complicated by contradictory information.

The embarrassed silence that followed Jacob's remark told me that the others were still uncomfortable with the death of the neighbor. As for me, I was just tired. I'd been driving most of the day, had only managed a short nap before heading out for the job, and was now driving again. Weariness just served to anesthetize my conscience, if I had one, which wasn't likely. Mac had done his best to amputate it. It was, he said, a handicap in our line of business.

Resisting the impulse to blast him, I replied, "Hell, I was just making conversation, Jacob. We all know you're good at your job. Nobody was questioning that."

Mollified, he mumbled, "Sorry, I was overreacting." I could feel the tension leave the car.

Just to cover all the bases, I said, "Nice shooting, Thomas."

Thomas was perhaps the more likeable of the group. He had a quiet air of confidence without the arrogance that so often develops in people who operate outside the law with immunity. He never said much unless there was a point to it. I had decided that I'd welcome him on any future team of mine, but I never got the chance - he went missing, presumed dead, a few months later. It should have been Jacob.

The other two were no prizes so far as I was concerned. Herman was still new enough in the business to be affected by his conscience - he kept looking at Jacob and me as though he was trying to discover where we hid the horns and tail. Brent was British, with that supercilious demeanor that I never could stand

120

and one that Americans often encountered in England. He seemed competent enough, but we cordially disliked one another - the British are polite enough - even though we were able to work together. Actually, to give him credit, I don't think I would have been able to carry it off as well as he did if the situation had been reversed and he was in charge.

In other words, it was a fairly typical team for our outfit.

The papers that Mac had provided for us were official enough that, when we were forced to travel on a main road, they got us through any checkpoints we happened upon. We had one bad moment outside Metz, near the French border, when one guard held us up while he made a radio call. It seemed to take him forever and we were about ready to shoot our way clear when he came back with our papers, apologized for the delay, and waved us through.

For the most part we stayed on back roads, stopping in small towns to eat and sleep. It's pretty country and, under other circumstances - say, no war and more desirable companionship - would have made for a great little vacation. All in all, my first mission into Germany was a little anticlimactic. Our biggest problem wasn't the enemy, but rather gasoline. It was in short supply and, while we had the proper authorization papers, all the papers in the world couldn't buy gas that didn't exist. More than once we were down to fumes, having exhausted even the three five-gallon jerry cans in the trunk, and several times we stopped at night to siphon some from a vehicle some poor soul had left unattended.

Four days after making our rendezvous, we were back in London, having left the Mercedes in the hands of the Resistance. I had gotten fond of the thing and hated to leave it, finding myself wondering just how I could afford one once the war was over. I wasn't one to bear grudges, assuming we won the war, and the Germans built some of the finest automobiles in the world.

After our debriefing with Mac, we left in different directions. After being cooped up together for so long, no one was anxious to have a celebration drink or dinner, including me. I did check with

Mac to see if Tina was in town, but she was still on her mission, whatever it was. I said to hell with it and went back to the base to see if I could set any records for sleeping.

Chapter 19

"Have you ever heard of Emil Taussig, Eric?"

As was standard in Mac's office, he used my code name. Also standard was the window behind his back, making it difficult to see his face, other than the startling black eyebrows framed by the carefully barbered gray hair. He wore his customary gray flannel suit - this one in a charcoal shade - a neat white shirt, a conservative silk tie and he may have looked like a well-preserved middle-aged banker or businessman to some people, but he'd never look like that to me. I happened to know that he was one of the half-dozen most dangerous and ruthless men in the world.

"I don't believe ... on second thought, I do remember something about him from my surveillance training class. Wasn't he the Jewish gentleman in Stalin's undercover apparatus? An expert in surveillance techniques?"

"He was, and still is, although he's carried it a step further." Mac pushed a folder across the desk to me. "Read, memorize and destroy. You'll find some interesting variations and proposals in there. I wouldn't mind having him on our team - or dead," he added grimly.

I looked up from the plain manila folder. I suppose in another office in another agency, it would have been marked *Top Secret*, but Mac didn't bother with such pompous nonsense - our whole operation would have been classified Top Secret, except that, for all practical purposes, we didn't exist - on paper at least.

"Dead?" I asked. "Are we going after Russians now?"

"Soviets, Eric," he said with a disapproving look. "Our besieged allies prefer that term. And no, we are not targeting Mr. Taussig, we are merely stealing one of his ideas. I doubt that the gentleman

- using the word advisedly - will object, even if he were to somehow discover this practical application of his theory."

"And that is ...?"

"Taussig has been advocating a multiple shadow technique as a substitute for open military action. The actual implementation of such a technique has been temporarily interrupted by Germany's invasion of the Soviet Union; however, if he survives, his ideas are going to prove troublesome to some countries, possibly including ours." Mac shook his head, whether in admiration or disgust, I couldn't tell. Knowing Mac, it could have been either.

I waited patiently for him to get to the point. It never did any good to try to hurry Mac and I had nothing else to do at the moment, anyway. I had just returned from the team assignment in Loewenstadt and had spent the last week sitting around, hoping to get a nice, quiet assignment by myself. I was fed up to here with the temperamental sons of bitches our business seemed to attract.

We'd always been kind of a lone-wolf outfit, myself in particular. The others probably didn't enjoy working with me any more than I did with them. Mac seemed to favor the type. He'd pointed out to me once, in this regard, that the Three Musketeers and their pal d'Artagnan were no doubt a swell bunch of fellows, and that the relationship between them was a beautiful thing, but that when you studied the record you came to the sad conclusion that Louis the thirteenth would have got a lot more for his money, militarily speaking, by hiring four surly swordsmen who wouldn't give each other the time of day. I remembered Mac saying that he made a point of keeping us dispersed as much as possible, to cut down on the casualties. "Break it up," he'd say wearily, "break it up, you damn overtrained gladiators, save it for the Nazis."

He finally continued. "Taussig's proposal was to cover all key politicians in a target country who weren't being properly cooperative. Every doubtful man or woman in public life was to be shadowed by an agent trained in homicide who would have orders to take his subject out instantly and permanently when the whistle blew. The resulting confusion and lack of leadership would then, presumably, enable the relatively peaceful subjugation of the country."

"It sounds almost workable, but the logistics would be a nightmare. If someone gets itchy fingers, the whole thing could collapse. Are we taking over a country?"

Mac gave me a cold smile at my sarcasm. "No, Eric" he said, "just a city."

I couldn't think of anything to say to that, so I just waited for him to continue.

"We're going to adapt Taussig's ideas in reverse - the idea is liberation rather than conquest - and on a slightly smaller scale. On the French coast there is a small port city called Cherbourg. Of no immediate importance at the present, it will become very important within the next few weeks. I am told that it is vital for our forces to take this city quickly, when the time comes; otherwise the Germans may have time to bring up reinforcements which could have a domino effect on the rest of the operation." Dryly, he added, "Those were the words used to explain the situation to me."

I reflected upon the implications of this information. We all knew that, sooner or later, we had to carry the ground war to France. From what Mac had said, it would happen sometime within the next few weeks and, I assumed, close to Cherbourg. I was, by now, so used to operating in the blind that I was unaccustomed to - not to mention uncomfortable - being told so much, especially information as sensitive as this.

Mac seemed to read my mind. With a thin smile, he said, "I thought you'd appreciate being privy to high-level strategies for a change." The smile disappeared. "You and Frank will be the only field agents aware of the scope of the mission, or it's importance. Assuming of course, that somebody else doesn't leak the information. We are going to have to use some of British Intelligence's people on this one."

I groaned inwardly. These interdepartmental missions had a habit of turning into disasters and the loss of Gene and Derek a few months before still left a bad taste in my mouth.

Mac saw my expression and said quietly, "We have no choice, Eric. The operation is too large for our limited resources."

"Yes, Sir. Ours but to do or die, and so forth. Okay, what do we do and who do we do it to?"

"We are going to take out two - and, wherever possible, three - levels of command in a single night. Frank will be in charge of our people and you, with your superior command of French and German, will be in charge of BI's people. You and Frank, with my limited input, will have a week to develop a plan of attack before you make rendezvous with your contact in France. Your targets - at least currently - are in the folder you have. Depending on how long it takes before you're given the go-ahead, some of the names may change due to transfers or leaves, but the position is the target, regardless of its current occupant. Any questions?"

That was his usual ending to a briefing, so I gave him mine.

"No, Sir," I said.

Chapter 20

The first time I saw her was at a dinner party, which I'd been instructed to attend in order to make contact with her. From the photo I had seen, she was almost unrecognizable, but it was Yvette, all right - expensive furs, cocktail dress and hairdo notwithstanding. I started to walk over and introduce myself when I saw her lift her left hand casually and gracefully to brush the long dark hair back from her ear. She wasn't looking at me, not even facing my way, and the movement was wholly natural; but I hadn't forgotten those grim months of training before they sent me out, and I knew the gesture was meant for me. I was seeing the sign we had that meant: *I'll get in touch with you later. Stand by.*

I'd almost broken the basic rule that had been drilled into all of us, never to recognize anybody anywhere. The stand-by signal meant business. It meant: *Wipe that silly smile off your face, Buster, before you louse up the works. You don't know me, you fool.* The problem was that she was *supposed* to know me. I was impersonating a Prussian nobleman and the cover story was that she had met me in Paris last Christmas and we would discover each other again at the party, but apparently something had changed.

I wandered around for a while, trying not to get involved in any extensive conversations. I did attract some attention, as Prussian Counts were not as numerous in Cherbourg as they were in Paris - a fact that had been counted on to get me an invitation to the party.

Eventually, the unwitting hostess - I forget her name - came toward me with Yvette in tow and introduced us. "Count Haufman, may I present Mademoiselle Devereaux? She has been dying to meet you."

Yvette extended her hand with a graciousness that made me want to click my heels, bow low, and raise her fingers to my lips - which I was supposed to do, of course, and did - and might have otherwise forgotten. This royalty business takes some practice. Her little finger moved very slightly in my grasp, in a certain way. It was the recognition signal, the one that asserted authority and demanded obedience.

I'd been expecting that. I looked straight into her eyes, not responding with the correct answering signal, which I knew perfectly, but instead returning the same signal, overriding hers. Her eyes narrowed very slightly, and she took back her hand. You get so you can recognize them, something that betrays them to one who knows. Even bathed and shampooed and perfumed, girdled and nyloned, Yvette had it. I could see it and recognize it because I had it myself.

The photograph I'd seen had depicted a rather scrawny young girl with short-cropped hair and a dirty face, someone this lovely young woman in front of me would have disdained to notice.

"Charmed to meet you, Mademoiselle," I said. Which was the literal truth.

"No, the honor is mine, Count Haufman," she replied. "We are so glad to welcome you here in our little city." I doubted it.

"Colonel, please," I said. I was, of course, in dress uniform. "The titles are so passé these days, are they not? And I appreciate your hospitality."

"Then you must call me Charlene."

"I will be happy to, if you will call me Rolf."

This was not just politeness, of course. It was the normal cloak and dagger games so loved by the intelligence people. I wasn't so sure that two people first introduced to each other would get so quickly to first names, but the identification routine had been based upon us having met before, though briefly. Fortunately we got no untoward glances from our hostess.

128

We took care of the obligatory pleasantries, in French of course. There was a trace of mockery in her dark eyes as she allowed herself to be led away by the hostess to meet someone else. I was struck by the color of her eyes, not blue, not green, but somewhere in between and very pale. They were the shade you sometimes see in the ocean where the water is shallow enough to mute the normal blue. I watched appreciatively as she walked away, swaying just a little more than necessary in her finery.

I glanced around quickly, back where I was watching myself every second to see how I was going over in the part I was playing, where every word I spoke could be my death warrant. I was no longer working my facial muscles automatically; the manual control center had taken over. I signaled for a smile and it came. I thought it was pretty good. I'd always been a fair poker player as a boy, and I'd learned something about acting later, with my life at stake.

I had a couple of drinks, happy to find good scotch at the bar, engaged in a few polite conversations, both in German and French, and was wondering what the hell to do next when I felt someone take my arm. The musical voice I heard earlier said, "You look so bored, Rolf. Let's walk out on the balcony and get some fresh air."

I let her lead me outside, to the far wall. It was perfect springtime weather, although it appeared we were the only ones enjoying it. The balcony - actually a second-floor patio - was large enough for a small party and we were far enough from the doorway to talk in private.

Her voice changed, becoming harder, although she continued to speak in French - I knew she spoke perfect English, but it was not the place for that language, even away from the crowd. I don't know whether she was being professional or just enjoyed the small advantage it gave here. My French was not nearly as good as my German, which was in keeping with my cover.

"I don't work for you," she spat.

I could play that game as well. "Not normally, you don't. But for the next two weeks or so, you will do as you're told. You can't give orders without knowing the whole situation, and that's *my* job" - well, mine and Frank's, but she didn't know that. I waited a minute, but she swallowed her next retort and remained silent.

Having made my point, I could afford to be magnanimous. In English, I continued, "Look, I didn't mean to be so abrupt. I didn't ask for this job, British Intelligence gave it to me, and we're going to have to work together for a little while. Why don't we just relax and enjoy it?" It wasn't totally a lie. BI had given the job to someone, who gave it to Mac, who gave it to me - and Frank.

She looked around quickly, although it was obvious that no one was within hearing distance of us. "Careful," she warned.

"It's okay, so long as we keep our voices down and smile a little. My French isn't that good, and we don't have much time. I don't want to misunderstand you or miss something critical."

"Very well," she agreed.

"Now, what's with the change in plan? You were supposed to recognize me from last Christmas."

"I know, but we had a new officer assigned as second-in-command to Colonel Kiersten, one who knows me."

"So?"

"He's here at the party. He was also with me at a party last Christmas, not in Paris, but in Marseille."

I had never been in Marseille, but I knew that it was on the Southern coast, about as far away from Paris as you can get and still be in France. "Good thinking. It's a good thing I haven't had a chance to tell that story to anyone. Which one is he?"

"The tall blond Colonel. His name is Franz Heinrich. The shorter, dark one is Colonel Kiersten."

"I know Kiersten from his picture. I'll pass the word about Heinrich. Anything else I need to know?"

"No, there are no other changes in command. Have you brought any new orders?"

She used the word *brought* deliberately, putting me in my place neatly, without leaving me room to object. I smiled wryly and she smiled back and we were friends - sort of.

"No, I didn't *bring* any new orders. I'm just here in case new orders are necessary and to help you out with Kiersten when the time comes, should you be out of position." I looked at her appraisingly. She was holding up well, but there were the telltale lines around the eyes and mouth and the look in the eyes that I had seen more often than I'd like. It was the far look, the knowing look of a young person forced to grow up too fast, to witness - and engage in - horrifying acts and events that normally would be alien to someone of such tender years. I'd seen eighteen-year-old kids with thirty-year-old eyes after a few months in combat. I used to look at myself in the mirror to see if I had that same look, but I couldn't tell. I think there was something left out of me, or I was born several hundred years too late. I was born for this kind of work, unlike most young people of my generation.

Yvette, however, had a slightly different look. The one that comes from too much partying, too many men and too much humiliation. She had been in the field too long, forced to endure too much, and it showed to someone who knows. I'm not criticizing - I felt very sorry for her. The worst assignments aren't the ones requiring you to do something nasty; the worst assignments are the ones demanding that you *be* something nasty, for weeks and months at a time. I knew the humiliation she must feel, seeing herself through the eyes of her fellow countrymen.

131

I'd seen her dossier, the parts that didn't include classified details, and knew that she had been a debutante in Paris before the war and had joined the Resistance after her father had been killed by the Germans. Somehow, Mac had recruited her, trained her, and sent her back into France as a double agent. British Intelligence thought she was working for them - which she was - but she also performed certain tasks for Mac. For the past two years she had been, to put it bluntly, a high-class French whore; the plaything of high-ranking German officers. What the supercilious dowagers and finger-pointing hypocrites didn't know was that, during that time, the information she had passed on to BI had saved countless lives. What even BI didn't know was that she was also responsible for nine touches, four of which she had accomplished herself. The others were set up by her for other agents.

She was acting in both capacities in Cherbourg. She was our pipeline into the German command structure here and was also under instructions to take out Colonel Kiersten if she was in position to do so. My secondary job was to provide her with a backup if the signal went up when she didn't have access to him.

In a way, she reminded me of Tina and a small pang of regret hit me as I remembered our week in London. We had made some tentative plans to meet later on, if we had the chance, and some definite plans to meet in Paris after the war.

I must have let some of my thoughts show on my face. Yvette brought me back to reality fast. "Damn you!" she hissed, her eyes flashing. "Don't you *dare* feel sorry for me!"

The transformation was startling. Instead of a little tired and gray and worn, she now looked young and savage and alive, and I realized that I had misjudged her. At least a part of what I had been reading in her face and eyes was due to excellent acting ability. In that moment I wondered if perhaps I had been somewhat hasty in feeling a little superior to her. She no longer looked like someone who had been forced by circumstances to use her talents as her country needed. I made a mental note to ask Mac exactly who had recruited whom. This girl was something special.

132

"I wasn't feeling sorry for you," I lied. "You just reminded me of someone else there for a moment."

Her eyes softened. "Ah," she said in French, "a long-lost love, perhaps?"

"Perhaps," I said. There's nothing like a story of lost love to soften up a female, especially a French female, but it made me feel a little guilty, using Tina in that way.

"It happens, especially in wartime. But one must go on." She paused a moment, perhaps reflecting on a memory of her own. Then she took a deep breath and I watched in fascination as her features relaxed back into the original mask I had first seen. She was as good as some of the celebrity-impersonators I had seen who could change characters at will.

"We'd better get back to the party before my Colonel gets jealous," she said, back to business-as-usual. "Come, I'll introduce you."

We went back inside and I spent the next hour observing the social amenities before I could get away.

All of our agents were now in place. In total, we had nine of ours, not counting Frank and me, and seven of BI's, counting Yvette as theirs. That made a total of sixteen individual targets. Only Frank and I knew the whole picture - even Yvette thought that Kiersten and the new second-in-command were the only targets. In an operation so large, it was impossible to select only agents who didn't know one another, so Frank and I had agreed upon a cover story. Each agent was told that his or her particular mission was in support of a secondary mission. In the event two or more agents recognized one another, we hoped they would each think the other was assigned to the secondary, less important mission. We hoped.

After finalizing our plans, I had spent the next three weeks briefing BI's agents and refreshing their training in the finer arts of surveillance techniques, while Frank did the same in London. BI provided the necessary papers for both groups and we infiltrated the agents into Cherbourg over a four-week period.

There are times in practically every operation when things come to a tired halt and there's nothing to do but wait patiently for them to get moving again. Finally, things got tense as the news of the Allied landing at Normandy shocked the Germans - and exhilarated the French - but it came as a relief to me. That information was no longer critical and I was just as happy not to worry about it.

In a way, it made our job that much easier. With the Germans looking over the hill - so to speak - for the enemy, they weren't so likely to look closer to home. Social activities were curtailed drastically, which let me off the hook - there were greater concerns than entertaining a minor Prussian nobleman. The next several days would have been mildly boring if it were not for the day-to-day possibility of someone making a mistake - including me. Every time a plane came near, I involuntarily looked up to see if it was the one.

Knowing that nerves would be frayed, I resisted the impulse to "fine-tune" the operation. They all knew their jobs and no purpose would be served trying to second-guess an agent - or even provide a friendly word of encouragement. These weren't schoolchildren, they were trained fighting men and women who knew their jobs as well as, if not better, than I. Unless something changed, and as things stood it was unlikely that anyone would be transferred or allowed leave, I had to stay as far away from the others as possible, even Yvette. If she needed to get in touch with me, she knew where I was. I spent a lot of time thinking about Tina, and - on occasion - Yvette, which just made me feel guilty. So, for the most part, I turned my mind off and read a lot and slept a lot.

One afternoon late in June, while I was sitting outside my hotel reading, a Messerschmidt flew toward the city, trailing smoke. I knew it was a Messerschmidt because I had been told it would be, not because I recognized it. As the plane passed overhead, a parachute opened as the pilot bailed out. Within a few seconds, the

134

plane exploded in a tremendous ball of flame and debris, accompanied by the thunderous roar of the explosion an instant later. Anyone in town would have to have been deaf not to hear it.

Well, that was the idea. Our biggest problem during the two weeks Frank and I had planned the operation had been the signal. We had to get word from the Allied Command that it was time to go, and then had to pass the word to sixteen agents. We couldn't have everyone walking around with a radio and tracking down that many people to personally pass the word simply wasn't feasible, not to mention mildly suspicious. We had to have a sure-fire signal that could not be misunderstood. If the timing was off or somehow a signal was accidentally duplicated - we'd toyed with the idea of ringing the church bell - the whole operation could fall apart. Frank had come up with the idea of flying one of our planes over the town and Mac had refined the idea into its present form. Where he got a Messerschmidt I have no idea. I'd wondered what the odds were of a real German pilot getting his plane shot up and heading for Cherbourg, but I'd been assured that we were out of the traffic pattern, to use some aerial terminology.

Satisfied that the signal had been sufficient, I waited until the pilot landed just outside town and walked back to my chair and opened my book - *War and Peace*, if it matters. I'd started it in college and had never finished it and I was now remembering why. The signal did not require an immediate response. Each target was left to the assigned agent's discretion. If he - or she - could make the touch discreetly with no witnesses and little chance of the body being discovered prematurely, he would do so as soon as feasible. Otherwise, we would each wait until nightfall and then pick the best time, with four o'clock in the morning being the deadline, by which time the job became critical, to be accomplished by any means, regardless of risk.

As I pretended to read, I hoped the pilot was as good an actor as Yvette. Mac couldn't resist a Machiavellian touch and the pilot was to bring the good news - for the Germans, of course - that the Allies were being pushed back into the Channel. He, and his companions in the *Luftwaffe* were winning the air battle and he, himself, had shot down three of the new American P-51B *Mustangs*, before being hit and, unable to steer, had ended up over Cherbourg.

This should be cause for celebration, making our jobs easier as well as lulling the Germans into a false sense of security, making the scheduled dawn assault more of a surprise. Sometimes I wondered if the war wouldn't have been long over if Mac had been in charge of it. You may have gathered by now that, in our outfit, no one went around grumbling about the "old man" not knowing what he was doing - although I understand that's a favorite pastime in the more traditional military units. If Mac had told us that there was a twenty percent chance we could end the war by parachuting into Berlin in broad daylight and making a direct assault upon the German Command Headquarters, we'd probably grab our guns and head for the nearest airplane, knowing he wouldn't ask us to do something he didn't believe in himself.

Not that Mac wouldn't send one of us out on a mission that was considered important enough to justify the death of an agent. If the mission was important enough and the chance of success good enough, he would accept it, even though the agent stood little chance of returning. But if that were the case, Mac would be the first to admit it. And, because of the loyalty and respect Mac commanded among his agents, not one of us would refuse to go.

As near as I could figure out later, somewhere between forty and sixty people died that afternoon and night, including all sixteen of our targets and two of my group. The latter two were forced to break in on a party in which both their targets, junior officers, were celebrating the supposed German victory along with their men. They were both found inside the house, along with seven dead Germans, including the two officers. They didn't know each other, to the best of my knowledge, so I don't know if they met outside, compared stories and went in together, or if they each went in separately. In either instance, they gave a good accounting of themselves.

The next day, we found Germans with broken necks, slit throats and small .22 caliber holes in various parts of their anatomy. Often, we found more than one German in the same spot, indicating a friend had been in the wrong place at the wrong time. However, most of the excess casualties came from a single occurrence. One of our agents, a man named Monk, had a thing about weapons that go bang in a big way. I remembered hearing the explosion around two o'clock that morning, but had been too busy myself to pay it much mind. As Frank told me later, Monk had wired the house of the Panzer Division Commander with explosives of his own devising and could have blown the building anytime after ten. However, the Commander was having his own celebration party, complete with female entertainment and, as people kept arriving, Monk simply waited for a full house and pressed the button. It was hard to tell how many people had been in the house after the explosion tore them apart.

I had met Monk once before and, if I'd known Frank was going to select him for this mission I would have advised against it. It was on the Hofbaden job that I was assigned the explosives expert we called Monk. He had hulking shoulders and an oddly sensitive, handsome face. He had an ascetic face that could light up with a burning enthusiasm when he got that fanatical look in his bright blue eyes. It was one of his biggest assets. He was damn convincing playing a dedicated Heil-Hitler boy. His rather squat, powerful body went oddly with his long, sensitive face, crisp dark hair, and brilliant blue eyes. There was nothing wrong with him physically, but he gave an impression of deformity nevertheless. He seemed to have been made of parts intended for several different men. I'd never decided whether Mac had picked that code name for him because he was built like a gorilla or because he often wore the expression of a saint, and I'd never asked. There had been more important things to worry about at the time. I'd have killed him if I hadn't needed him, the murderous bastard. It was a perfectly simple job, but he wanted to make a wholesale massacre of it. He got his kicks from blowing up people in bunches instead of one at a time. He came under the heading of the kind of unfinished business we normally try not to leave behind us. I mean, it's only in the movies that you make bitter enemies in one scene and let them live to raise hell with you in the next. If Monk had been an enemy agent, I'd have shot him dead the instant I had no further use for him, as a simple act of self-preservation. As it was, I'd brought him back to base alive, knowing that I was probably making a mistake, and that it was a mistake the Monk himself would never have made. I'd got to know the guy pretty well - as well as you can get to know a guy you've risked your life with and beat hell out of.

In a technical sense, Monk was a very good man. He was a genius in the field of high explosives, where my own knowledge is less than adequate. The only trouble was, he just loved to see things blow, particularly if the things had people in them. Personally, if I'm assigned to get one man, I like to get that man. This business of demolishing a whole landscape with figures - even enemy figures - just to erase a single individual seems pretty damn inefficient to me. As the agent in charge, I'd had to lean on Monk pretty hard to make him do things my way. He wasn't the man to forget it.

Well, he'd got to see another pretty building blow up with lots of people inside, including a few relatively innocent bystanders - not that that mattered to him - and when we got back to London, I told Frank about the Hofbaden incident, for what it was worth. Monk had been under his command and it was his decision what to put in his report to Mac.

Anyway, as I have indicated, I was rather busy when Monk's explosion occurred. I had had a hell of a time locating Colonel Kiersten. He wasn't in his house and neither was Yvette. I finally found someone who told me she had seen him and Yvette walking down toward the beach. As I headed in that direction I heard the boisterous sounds of a party or two - apparently Mac's stratagem had worked - and, in the distance, sounds of gunfire. I never did find out if the gunfire was from one of our agents or simply Hans or Friedrich letting off a little celebratory steam. Apparently, no one else was curious enough to investigate either, and the mission was going off like clockwork, thanks to Mac's little embellishment.

138

It was about then that Monk's explosion went off, which seemed a little extreme for a celebration, but I had a job to do. I was reasonably sure that Yvette would take care of it for me, but my job was to make sure. As I got near the rocky beach, I saw a lone figure walking from the water toward a small beach house, his silhouette clearly visible in the moonlight. As he approached the light streaming from the open door of the beach house, I recognized Kiersten a moment before he called out in German.

"Charlene, my pet, what's taking you so long?" He held his arms out as though expecting her to run into them.

I was still in the shadows and I knew he couldn't see me with the bright light in his eyes, so I pulled out my Woodsman, intending to finish the job right then. Before I had a chance, there was a small, solid thud, the sound of something hard and sharp burying itself in something moderately soft. Well, to be honest, I'm not that good at sounds; I'd caught the glint of the throwing knife before it struck. Kiersten's mouth opened, but no scream came out, just a barely audible - at my distance - gasp of pure agony. Then there was a rattle of dislodged stones beside him as she ran from the side of the beach house and threw an arm around his neck while the other hand groped for and found the weapon buried under the armpit, wrenched it free, and drove it home a second time. By the time I reached her, she'd laid him down and was squatting beside him, wiping her blade on his shirt. She looked up at me. Her eyes were strange and shiny; for a moment she was just another dangerous predator crouching over its kill, not quite human. Or very human, depending upon your definition of humanity.

She was a unique specimen in a world of tender ladies who couldn't bear the thought of guns or violence. Keeping her leashed would be an offense against nature, like calling a beagle off a rabbit or asking a good pointer to ignore a covey of quail.

"So?" she whispered.

I didn't feel it was the right time to point out that she'd been very lucky that the German hadn't screamed; and that we don't like that throwing-knife routine even when silence is not important. There's a lot of bone in a human body, and slipping a blade accurately between the ribs is difficult enough at contact range. From ten or twelve feet away, it's strictly a game of chance.

"You did fine," I said.

"Bullshit! I got lucky. I was planning to take him at the house, but he came in all excited and insisted that we go out for dinner. This knife was the only weapon I could get my hands on. I carry it in my purse all the time - for protection, I told him. He thought it was cute, the sexy little French girl with the sexy little knife."

Actually, on second look, the knife did seem a little sexy, with the pretty carved hilt and the etched steel blade. I hadn't noticed before - a weapon that has just killed a man looks deadly to me, always.

She seemed to feel the need to explain something to me. Well, a talking jag is a fairly common reaction after a kill, especially among women. Yvette continued, "He used to make me dress up in a *femme fatale* getup, with the knife slid down in my stocking. It turned him on. We would pretend that I was trying to kill him and he would take the knife away from me and hold it to my throat or stomach while he made love to me. He also liked to cut me, just a little."

She took a deep breath. "Look at me, chattering away like an amateur." She smiled wryly. "Anyway, I thought it was a sort of poetic justice, to kill the pig with this knife that he liked so much."

"Sure," I said, "I understand." Actually, I did. In this business, it's not often that you get to kill someone you hate, and we're human - regardless of opinions to the contrary. When revenge and duty go hand in hand, why not enjoy it? Tina had taught me that.

"The job got done, that's what counts," I added, softly, looking down at her. Then she stood up and I really looked at her as a person. She was quite pretty in her one-piece swimming suit, still a little wet and revealing the small swell of her erect nipples. I saw her eyes change as she watched me staring at her and I remembered another common reaction after a kill - common to both men and women.

She took a small step toward me and whispered, "It would be a shame to waste this lovely beach house on such a beautiful night, wouldn't it Eric?"

I tried to think of a suitably flippant reply, but my mouth was suddenly dry. I just moved forward and picked her up and carried her inside....

Afterward, we lay there feeling luxuriously relaxed after the long tension. She was smoking a cigarette I lit for her, after pouring two glasses of Kiersten's favorite Margaux. I wasn't much of a red wine fan, but this tasted pretty good. Perhaps I just hadn't spent enough money before.

Finally, I had gone out and dragged the body around the side of the house, thankful that nobody had come by. When I came back, Yvette had refilled our glasses. As I sat down on the bed beside her, she turned to me with a strange look on her face. "Who was she, Eric?" she asked gently, "This Tina, that you love so much?"

I stopped with the wine glass halfway to my mouth. I frowned at her, then remembered my momentary lapse in the throes of passion, so to speak.

"I'm sorry, Yvette," I said, "it was just a slip of the tongue." She didn't seem to be upset, just mildly curious. "I wouldn't exactly call it love - we only spent two weeks together, a couple months ago. I guess it was just so recent, that I'm still used to using her name."

"Who's kidding who?" she laughed. "I'm a woman, and I'm French. I know when a man is in love." She held up her hand. "Don't try to spare my feelings, Eric. I am not so fragile, especially now. Besides," she went on, "you're not really my type. I've got a sweet young man waiting for me in London. After the war, we will be married, and I'll tell him some beautiful lies about my thrilling adventures as a courier for the Resistance, and how I stayed true to him, and he will tell me some beautiful lies and we will live happily ever after."

I had to laugh at her practical approach to life. She was doing what she could for her country and then she would do what she could for her husband. It was a typically French attitude. "And I'm just a temporary diversion, is that it?" I asked with a grin.

"Just so. And a very beautiful diversion." She stubbed out her cigarette and drank the last of the wine in her glass. Lying back in the bed, she opened her arms and said, "Come here, Diversion, I am not through with you yet."

She wasn't.

We stayed in the beach house until dawn when the troops arrived. Within a few hours Cherbourg was liberated, so I guess you could call the mission a success. We took a couple of days getting back to London, where Yvette promptly disappeared with her boyfriend, and a couple more days reporting to Mac. I never found out if the Taussig technique was used again - at least I wasn't involved if it was - but I had my suspicions on at least two other occasions. Mac wasn't the type to pass up a winning strategy.

Chapter 21

While things were being sorted out following the invasion of France, I had some free time, but Tina was off on another mission. I had a feeling Mac was planning things that way, but was afraid to ask him - he might have told me the truth. After a few days I got bored and reported back to the camp just in time to be grabbed for instructor duty. As the pace of the war increased, and our casualties mounted, Mac was recruiting and training faster, and more of it was being done here in Britain. In between assignments we occasionally filled in to help out.

I didn't mind it. Actually, I got a kick out of teaching the finer points of sniping and knife work. I was more effective now, having gained some insight by practicing in the field. I found that there's nothing like a few close calls to sharpen your teaching techniques, and the students tend to pay more attention to someone who's been there and done it. Theory is all well and good, but I think our educational system would be better off if the teachers and professors were forced to practice their trade for a few years before they were allowed to teach it.

In addition to the new recruits, there were a few oldtimers like myself at the base, mostly between assignments. There were some new faces I hadn't seen before and a couple more that I *had* seen and wasn't particularly interested in seeing again. From their reactions they weren't interested in renewing old acquaintances either. That was the normal attitude at the base - you would walk into the canteen and find a couple of tables full with the latest training class, and the rest of the tables occupied by one or, at most, two diners. Oh, we still had a few agents who liked to socialize but, for the most part, we had all learned the futility of developing a friendship with people that might very likely be dead or missing the next time you heard their name mentioned, or whom you might have to leave behind on some mission.

There was one exception, one of Mac's first recruits - the class before mine - named Smitty. Smitty was on permanent administrative duty, the only one of us - "us" meaning field agents - who was. Smitty's job was to coordinate the information coming in on what were referred to as "standing targets" - people that Allied Command wanted eliminated but whom we hadn't gotten around to yet or weren't considered important enough for an assigned target. Mac had expanded this information and instituted a new procedure the previous year, in what he called the "recognition room," in response to developments in both Germany and the Soviet Union. Apparently, Mac's approach to warfare was no longer unique - not that it ever had been. Our profession had roots going far back in history, but in modern times, it was not the sort of profession one talked about or - heaven forbid - officially sanctioned.

Very handy fellows to have around, we killers. You can feel fine and self-righteous about disapproving of us when you don't need us; and you can feel fine and self-righteous about handing us medals when you do - provided we're wearing uniforms. If you don't wear a uniform and pick a specified individual on which to practice your trade, then everyone shudders and screams bloody murder. Someone once pointed out that the Victorians had a thing about sex but had no big problems with death, but modern civilization seems to have it reversed. Well, I told you I had been born a couple of centuries too late.

Actually, although you won't hear the word used too often - Mac likes the word "remover" - the correct terminology for our type of work is "assassin." I did some research once on the subject. It seems there was this bloodthirsty priest or lama or guru or whatever the word was back then, living up in the rocks of ... well, I don't remember where, but it was somewhere in the Middle East. He was called "The Old Man of the Mountain" and had a kind of religion, a murderous kind of religion, and a bunch of fanatic followers. He fed them hashish and sent them out to kill. Over time, they were called *Hashishin*, which eventually became *assassin*. That's where the word came from.

Anyway, the Germans and Soviets both had developed their own little bureau of assassins and Mac was now compiling files on them as information became available from the field, British Intelligence and God knows where else. Sometimes I wondered if Mac didn't have his own intelligence network in place, unknown to us and our allies. I wouldn't put it past him and some of his information was so accurate as to be frightening, such as the file on the General's neighbor on one of my previous missions.

I suppose the British had some people more or less engaged in our specialty, but we never saw anything on them. However, Mac had amassed a lot of information on the Soviet and German agents in our line of work, including photographs and sketches where available. The Soviet agents, being our allies, were included ostensibly so we could avoid killing one if we ran into him or her in the field. Actually, Mac had once hinted to me that the Soviet files would come in handy after the war. He had no faith that we would continue to be allies after the reason for our collaboration, Germany, was out of the picture.

The German agents, however, - along with the "standing targets" - all carried standing orders: "Terminate on sight, mission allowing." As the information in the recognition room grew, Mac needed someone to coordinate it and brief us field agents whenever we were on base. That's where Smitty came in. Smitty was probably the only one other than Mac who knew us all. He was invariably friendly and helpful; whenever we got back to base and he saw us in the canteen, he would limp over to say hello and discuss our recent mission, offering congratulations or condolences as indicated. Even the most obnoxious agent liked, or at least tolerated, Smitty, even though there was a downside.

Smitty limped because he didn't have much in the way of feet. They had been operated on drastically by some gentlemen in search of information. Various other parts of Smitty were also missing and there were scars that didn't make him very pleasant to look at.

Mac had given him the job upon his discharge from the hospital - Smitty's backup team had rescued him, albeit a little late - since he was obviously no longer fit for field duty. Don't think for a moment it was just a generous gesture towards a disabled employee. Part of it was, of course, that Smitty had successfully completed his mission before the previously mentioned gentlemen had caught him - Mac wasn't much more tolerant of failure than were the Nazis, and if Smitty had
gotten caught before completing the mission, he would undoubtedly have been sent back to the states.

But the main reason for Mac's decision was that we all had to check with the recognition room before we went out on assignment; we all had to see Smitty therefore, before every job. It was an antidote for optimism and overconfidence, since it was well known that Smitty had been as good as any of us, in his time. He'd just been a little careless, once...

On the other hand, it was nice to have someone with whom we could talk freely without worrying about compromising classified information or revealing too much about ourselves. All in all, it balanced out, because Smitty was also an antidote to the loneliness of the profession, an occupational hazard that both Smitty and Mac were well aware of. Someone had once remarked to me that if Smitty had not existed, it would have been necessary to invent him.

Chapter 22

As often happens during instructor duty, it was cut short by a summons from Mac.

"I suppose you've heard of the new German missiles, Eric?" he asked as I sat down. Actually, I hadn't, which gives you an idea of how insulated we were at the base. If someone there had heard of them, they hadn't bothered to inform me.

"No, Sir," I said. "I know a missile is something you throw or shoot, if that's what you mean."

"The Germans have carried the concept a step further. They've come up with a self-propelled missile which they are calling a 'V-Missile.' Apparently, it's a kind of flying bomb with a new kind of rocket motor attached, sort of like the sky-rockets you see on Independence Day. According to the experts, it will revolutionize warfare as we know it, if perfected."

He paused a moment, warming up to his subject. "The things have at least the range of a bomber, but smaller, faster and almost impossible to detect, let alone intercept. They are being fired from inside Germany-occupied territory and exploding here in England with no advance warning. The first ones started about three weeks ago."

The implications were staggering. I could see why someone was concerned. It was a quantum leap, on a par with the invention of the bow, replacing the less efficient spear, or the more modern invention of the firearm to replace the bow. Well, people have always had a nasty habit of inventing a better way of killing other people when the need arose.

When I was a boy I dreamed of owning a certain legendary weapon: the old Colt single action army revolver, in .45 caliber of course. It took some doing since there wasn't much money and, while my parents weren't opposed in principle to having meat providers like deer rifles and duck guns on our modest New Mexico ranch, they still clung to the European notion that while a weapon fired from two hands might be morally acceptable, a one-hand gun just had to be inherently evil; a distinction I still fail to comprehend. But I was a hardworking young fellow and a persistent one; and in the end I wound up defending myself from a lot of hostile tin cans and savage paper targets, not to mention a few ferocious jackrabbits, with my faithful, .45 Colt, only to discover that it wasn't all that great. Its accuracy left a lot to be desired, the leaf springs kept breaking under hard use, it was slow to load and unload and, since it had to be cocked for each shot, not very fast to shoot.

The old six-shooter and its more durable and deadly successors had solved the violent problem that had brought it and them into existence only to leave society saddled with more and greater problems, leaving people wishing they could make them go away. The character who finds a way of uninventing the inventions that folks decide not to like is going to make a fortune. In the meantime, we've got the good old weapons syndrome of bigger, better and more deadly. In a way, this missile idea was the next logical step, given that an airplane is a terribly inefficient and expensive - not to mention dangerous - method of delivering a bomb. Why not have the bomb deliver itself?

Mac was waiting for my reaction, so I gave it to him. "It sounds like our side might be in trouble, Sir. How accurate are these V-Missiles?"

He nodded as though that was the logical question, which of course it was. "So far, not very. They've got to calculate the trajectory from the firing point, which doesn't leave a lot of room for errors. From what I was told, this first version kind of drops at random, creating more morale problems than actual damage. The Germans are finalizing the second version, called the 'V-2,' which will be more powerful, and should go into production within a couple of months. Even though it will be faster and carry a larger bomb, it is not substantially more accurate."

I took advantage of his pause to clarify a thought. "From what you're saying, Sir, these new missiles are not that effective. They may be scary, but it seems to me that their bombers are more deadly. At least they have a better chance of hitting the right target."

He nodded again. I was making the right responses. "You're right, Eric," he said. "However, you're missing the point. Hitler doesn't know that *we* know about the missiles and their limitations. It seems that he was relying upon their scare value, which may very well have succeeded, if we hadn't found out about them in time. After all, bombs falling out of the sky with no warning can be very demoralizing, and he was hoping to scare Britain, and possibly us, to sue for peace rather than face the supposed destruction these missiles could wreak."

"Giving him time to perfect them, I gather?"

"Exactly. Now that we know about the missiles, that won't work. There are only two ways these missiles could affect the war effort. One is for Germany to produce and fire enough of them to blanket his targets. That won't happen, for two reasons: We know they have production problems which are limiting their output; and the missiles have to be fired from a fixed launch site, which we can locate and put out of commission with our long-range bombers."

He waited for my obvious question, so I obliged him.

"And the second way is to improve the accuracy?"

He nodded at me once more. I was a prize pupil. Actually, none of it had been that difficult to figure out, once the concept had been explained.

"So I'm told. We've just recently discovered the existence of a team working on a 'V-3' version with some sort of homing device built in, based upon a miniaturized radar device. The Germans have an expert in radar who seems to feel that he can develop a system small enough to fit in a missile, and powerful enough to control the flight of the missile. I didn't understand half of what our expert told me, but apparently this new type of radar can determine it's own location - latitude and longitude - with sufficient accuracy to pinpoint a specific building, as opposed to the existing versions which have a hard time finding a whole city."

I was suitably impressed - frightened might be closer to the truth - and asked, "Can he actually do it?"

Mac shrugged. "Our experts admit it's possible, although we are some time away from the necessary technology. Our information is that even some German scientists are skeptical, but that may be just professional jealousy. The point is that we can't take the chance. If the 'V-3' works and is put into production, we may just lose this war."

After a reflective pause, I asked, "Who is this expert, and what am I supposed to do to him?" I mean, the background was nice, but I hadn't heard any orders yet and Mac was being just a little too accommodating with all this information. I had a feeling the other shoe was about to drop.

"We don't know."

It dropped. I started to point out, sarcastically, that intelligence work was not my forte, but Mac already knew that. The more I dealt with him the better I knew the way his mind worked. If he was going to ask me to do something like that, he would have approached it differently. So I just waited.

His lips twitched as if he wanted to smile. "However," he said, "we *do* know who *does* know. According to BI, one of his lab workers - a woman who calls herself Frieda - has offered to defect and help us to 'rescue' the good doctor from his own folly."

"You mean 'rescue' as in kidnap? I thought we didn't do much of that anymore."

"Don't be tiresome, Eric. Have I ordered you to kidnap anybody?"

"Oh," I said. "I see. At least I think I see," I added. Someone was being clever.

"It seems this young woman is also the doctor's mistress and is still rather fond of him, even though he is 'subverting his talents for an evil purpose,' as she put it. She will help us only on the condition that the doctor is not harmed."

I curled my lip. "One of those. Guns are okay, missiles are not. And she's willing to betray her lover and turn him into a traitor, so long as he's not harmed. What did British Intelligence say?"

"BI is convinced she is telling the truth and has promised her that both she and the doctor will be brought to London."

I thought that over and concluded that British Intelligence was not going to be happy, a fact which Mac immediately confirmed. "Although we often help out BI, we do not take orders from them, and a promise by them is not binding upon us."

Actually, knowing Mac, if the success of a mission was at stake, I doubted if any promise was binding. He was perfectly capable of looking you right in the eye and lying his head off.

He continued, "I have been advised that a kidnapping would not only be practically impossible, given the circumstances, but would probably convince the Germans that they are on the right track. On the other hand, the doctor must not be allowed to continue his research."

"So he's an assigned target?" I asked.

"In a manner of speaking. A direct touch might also let the Germans know we are aware of their efforts and consider them dangerous. It was thought that a nice, quiet suicide would be the perfect solution, especially since Frieda indicated that the doctor's last model was less than successful. He might be considered to be depressed over his failure, if it's set up right."

"Did the woman indicate he was depressed?"

"Actually, she said that the failure gave him a new idea which he considers very promising, but is not sharing with his colleagues until he has a working model. Fortunately, that buys us a little time to set it up."

I still wasn't sure I had the entire picture. "A suicide is not the easiest thing to set up, especially with a peace-loving mistress around who is apparently determined to protect her lover."

"My thoughts exactly," Mac agreed. "Therefore, your orders are to make contact with the woman, gain her trust and persuade her to identify the doctor and his location. You will then take the necessary steps to deal with him, and her if the situation warrants it. If you can arrange a convincing suicide, that would be nice; however an accident, some sort of medical problem - fatal of course - or even a lovers' quarrel resulting in homicide and subsequent suicide on her part are perfectly acceptable solutions. I will leave it to your discretion so long as the cause of death cannot be linked in any way to our side. Is that clear?"

"Yes, sir," I said.

Chapter 23

My target was a relatively unknown scientist who had been instrumental in developing radar technology for the Germans. He had been part of the research team - the major part, to hear him tell it - and had been cheated out of his proper recognition by the egomaniac who was in charge of the team and took all the credit. That was his version and it may have been the truth. His name was Doctor Hans Krueger - he insisted on the "Doctor" - and was a Doctor of Physics. He was also a posturing, egotistical loudmouth full of his own self-importance. He felt he was finally going to get the recognition that he so richly deserved and was willing to tell me almost anything to get it.

I couldn't have picked a better cover. The elaborate papers Mac had arranged to prove my identity had, so far, been a waste of time. Once Frieda introduced me as a writer for the Propaganda Ministry who had been assigned to do a feature story on the famous Doctor Krueger, I couldn't shut the guy up. He waved aside my proffered ID and invited me in as though we were old friends.

I had run into the type often in my pre-war newspaper career. There are some people who just live for the limelight. You break out a camera and you're lucky to get out of the room with any film left unexposed, or open up a notebook and they'll tell you their life story. This specimen wanted it so badly he was almost salivating.

Dr. Krueger may have been a genius; physically, however, he was unimposing. About five-six and at least a hundred and seventy pounds, he was a middle-aged butterball with thinning brown hair and a Hitler-like brush moustache which only served to emphasize his weak chin and thin lips. You might be reminded of your local baker who was overly fond of his own products until you got to the eyes. They were sunk into the fleshy face and not particularly noteworthy until you got close. Then you saw the piercing intelligence in the cold blue eyes with that contempt for lesser beings that comes not so much from a superior intellect as from a lifetime of being an object of ridicule. I mean, you put that much brainpower in a body which looked like his and you could almost write the story of his childhood. No wonder he was so thirsty for recognition - it would be his revenge on every girl who ever laughed at him and all the bullies who chased him home as a child.

I figured the best thing to happen to him had been Frieda. Not that she was a raving beauty, but she had that girl-next-door look the novelists like - light brown hair worn down to her shoulders, matching brown eyes and rather average features which nonetheless added up to an impression of prettiness. Actually, having met her first, Krueger's appearance was that more surprising. If I had met him first, I would have expected a dowdy, spinsterish woman with thick glasses and a preference for sturdy shoes and dark, formless clothes. Instead, Frieda was only a few years older than my twenty-five and looked and dressed more like a college student than a lab assistant.

I wondered briefly what she saw in him, but it was obvious. Some women are oblivious to the physical appearance of men, judging them on intellect alone. I'm not stupid by any means, but no one ever called me a genius, either, and I remembered a girl I had fallen madly in love with during my freshman year at college. In a way, Frieda reminded me of her. The girl, Laura, was also a freshman and I tried for weeks to talk her into going out with me. When she finally accepted, I found out it was only to have me introduce her to a professor with whom I had become friends through the fencing team. The professor was one of the ugliest men I have ever met, with a face that looked like it had gone several rounds with Joe Louis. He had two loves in life - well, three, after meeting Laura - fencing and the more abstract forms of mathematics having to do with quantum mechanics or something like that.

By the time I left the college - due to a little fracas involving a knife that I've previously mentioned - Laura had quit school and married the professor and was producing a bevy of ugly children. I hoped for their sake they also inherited their father's brains - it seems somehow unfair to go through life both ugly and stupid. I'm being a little unfair - Laura wasn't stupid, she just seemed that way compared with her husband. I never did figure out what they saw in one another and I didn't bother trying with Frieda and the doctor.

I had made contact with her the previous day, at the small apartment she maintained, per my instructions. I introduced myself as Heinrich Schumann from the Propaganda Ministry for the benefit of any neighbors who might be listening. She invited me in, her manner uncertain - she hadn't been notified of my cover.

It was obvious she was under a great deal of tension. Well, becoming a traitor to your country might be a rather tense experience. Actually, I never trust traitors, no matter how noble their proclaimed motives may be. A man, or a woman, who'll betray once, will betray twice. It didn't seem likely that anyone would go to all this trouble just to lure me - well, one of Mac's people - here and she was probably exactly what she said she was, but I checked anyway.

I said softly in German, "Hello, Frieda, please call me Eric. I believe we had an appointment." If anybody else was listening, that should sound innocent enough, while still identifying myself to her. I put my finger to my lips to warn her to be quiet, and quickly searched the apartment. Nobody else was hidden in the apartment and I couldn't spot any obvious listening devices, not that I expected to - if anyone was interested enough to plant any bugs, I wouldn't be able to find them and they probably knew too much already for me to worry about it.

Frieda's eyes cleared, impressed with my caution. "Yes, Eric, your friend told me you were coming. He explained to you what I want?"

"Yes, he did." That wasn't a lie - I didn't say I planned to follow through with it, just that it was explained.

"Tell me how."

I hesitated a moment. Now it was the time to lie, but a good lie should follow the truth as much as possible; it makes remembering the lie easier. I decided to tell her the exact truth about procedures, and ignore the fact that the escape plan only allowed for one person, not three.

"How we manage to deal with your doctor friend will depend on who he is, where he is and what information you provide," I explained. "The second part, getting out of Germany and into London has already been set up. We will need a vehicle. If you or the doctor have one, fine; otherwise, I will steal one. There is a certain city not far from here where we will become French citizens, complete with papers. From there we will travel across France through a series of safe houses which have been used for the last two years to smuggle downed British aviators back to England."

"What are these safe houses?" she asked.

"They are mostly homes or businesses owned by members of the French Resistance and their sympathizers. They provide shelter, rest and food before going on to the next one."

"Where are they located? And which city do we go to first?"

I looked her in the eyes. "I'm sorry, I can't tell you that."

She didn't buy it. "I must have more information if I am to trust you."

I shrugged. "I am not authorized to tell you. If something should happen and you or the doctor get caught, the Gestapo is very good at obtaining information. I cannot risk jeopardizing the safety of dozens, perhaps hundreds of our friends in France for the sake of one girl's suspicions."

"But I will find out anyway, once we start."

I had an answer for that one, too. "No you won't. You will be blindfolded to and from each safe house."

I could see her considering what I had said. I waited. The easiest way to blow a lie is to try to oversell it.

I could see she still had some doubts. Some people are like that. I could understand it because I'm the same way. Sometimes, no matter how logical and straightforward somebody seems, I find myself thinking, *What is this sonofabitch trying to sell me and why?* It's a survival trait among professionals. There are times when you have to throw the numbers out and go on instinct. You learn to trust your judgment of people when you have to gamble your life on that judgment.

She asked the right question. "What about you? What if you get caught, are you so brave that you can't be forced to talk?" There was a hint of scorn in her voice.

I had three options. I could tell her the hell with her and walk out, hoping she'd stop me. I could tell her how we're trained to stand up under torture and withhold information, which would have been a lie. I had a feeling that I'd better tell the truth, which probably sounded more unbelievable than the first two approaches.

I shook my head. "No one is that brave, Frieda. Given enough time, anybody can be broken. In my organization we operate under a different set of rules. Depending on the circumstances, we are either allowed to say anything we want, or we are expected not to be captured alive."

She looked at me appraisingly. With her natural suspicions, if she'd been a professional I wouldn't have been able to sell it. But she'd never had to put her life on the line before.

"How?" she asked. But I could tell she'd decided to trust me, and the question was more curiosity than anything else.

I didn't pretend to misunderstand her. I reached up, never mind where, and removed the little pill we carry. Holding out my hand to show her, I said, "It's potassium cyanide, in pill form. One bite and it takes about twenty seconds. I understand that it's a pretty rough twenty seconds, but at least it's quick."

She was silent for a few seconds, making no attempt to pick up the pill. "His name is Doctor Hans Krueger," she finally said. "He lives ..." She gave me the address. I should have been congratulating myself. I had done exactly what I had been ordered to do, and done it well. After all, I was a pro. I do what I'm told, with a few exceptions; and if it means deceiving gullible little girls, that's just too damn bad. So why did I feel so shitty?

Chapter 24

I looked down at the two bodies on Krueger's living room floor. I try to make a point of this - if you can do it, you can damn well look at it. It was two-for-one day for good old Eric. She looked kind of small and innocent, lying there. The five bullet holes in her upper chest and neck looked oddly obscene and out of place. I didn't feel much for him - he was a valid target, performing work for his country which would harm mine - but she was simply a pawn in the game whose only fault was being too squeamish about what her lover was doing. Well, my orders had been quite clear, which didn't erase the bad taste in my mouth. Mac should be happy with the end result, even if it hadn't gone exactly as I had planned.

I bent over and picked up the gun she had pulled out of her jacket pocket. The little gun had two stubby black barrels; actually a solid, gun-shaped little block of metal bored with two holes, one above the other. A small curved butt that, with a hand of any size, wouldn't accept a full complement of fingers. If you held the gun normally, the pinky would be left waving in the breeze; but you don't shoot a derringer normally. You lay your trigger finger along the barrels, and point it at the cheating sonofabitch across the poker table, and pull the trigger with the middle finger.

The old-time gamblers wore them up their sleeves, or maybe in special leather-lined pockets of their embroidered waistcoats. The best-known specimens came in .41 caliber, throwing a big blob of lead without much velocity or accuracy; but how much do you need across a pile of marked cards? Incidentally, the derringer was first invented or at least popularized, we're told, by a guy named Deringer. Nobody seems to know where the extra "r" came from.

I put it in my pocket and stood there a minute, deciding the best way to set it up. I had been more or less playing it by ear up to this point. Frieda had confirmed that the doctor would not voluntarily defect and had also confirmed that he was in perfect health - I had asked, ostensibly because of the long trip ahead and the necessity to drug him.

After meeting Krueger, I had discarded the idea of suicide - nobody would believe that a guy with an ego like that would kill himself. That had left two options suggested by Mac - a lovers' quarrel or some sort of accident. Given Frieda's suspicious nature, I had concluded that any solution leaving her alive would compromise security, contrary to Mac's instructions. Actually, I had pretty much known all along that Mac expected the assignment to include two targets, not one, and had left it to my discretion only because there might be a small chance of dealing with the doctor without arousing the girl's suspicions.

During the interview with Krueger, it had become clear that I was not going to have much time to do any planning. After I had indicated to him that I had been briefed on his current work, he had pulled out his notes and tried to explain to me just how he had solved the major problems. I had nodded at the appropriate points, more out of politeness than any understanding of what he was saying. The key point, however, had been that he was ready to start work on the new model, which included sharing his ideas with his colleagues, starting the next day.

That had been the deciding factor. I had all the ingredients at hand, so why wait? My intention had been to shoot the doctor first and then Frieda, setting it up to look as though she had committed suicide after shooting her lover. It would require leaving behind my Woodsman, but I saw no choice. I suppose a psychiatrist would rub his hands in glee at the implications of my worrying about losing an inanimate hunk of metal when faced with the task of shooting two human beings, but it's been my experience that most professionals, in any field, become attached to the tools of their trade.

I had miscalculated the extent of Frieda's natural paranoia. As I stood up and reached behind me to pull the Woodsman from my belt, she jumped up from the chair and leaped in front of Krueger, who was standing by his desk. She already had the derringer out and pointed towards me - I think she sensed my decision, or saw it in my eyes, as I made it.

If she had been a professional, I would have been dead right then, but she had apparently never even fired it before, as she was straining on the trigger, completely surprised by the pressure needed to fire the ridiculous little gun. She started to bring up her other hand to help, but by then it was too late. I had more than enough time to bring my own pistol up and think the situation through - hell, even if I waited for her to fire the little monster, using both hands, the chances of her hitting anything while struggling against that incredible mainspring were practically nonexistent.

It had been the idea of a lovers' quarrel - my original idea - that had led to the next logical progression, given the then changed situation. Obviously, Frieda couldn't shoot herself from across the room - a suicide required powder burns - so who else would shoot her? Since it couldn't be an enemy agent, it would have to be a jealous lover, a third party. As the thought had occurred to me, I'd put it into action - surprised that she hadn't yet got her other hand on the gun. Aiming just above the outstretched derringer, I'd started firing, letting the pistol drift upwards and to the right a little with each shot. The first five bullets had gone into her upper chest and neck, and the last four continued the diagonal pattern, two going into Krueger's neck and face and the final two missing them both altogether. As they had fallen, I could see that, as I had hoped, at least two bullets had penetrated her neck and entered the doctor's chest. . . .

With a little push in the right direction, it was a perfect set-up. There was no evidence of a struggle, no weapons on either Frieda or the doctor to confuse the issue - just the picture of a brave woman trying to shield the doctor from her jealous lover and both of them getting shot by a panicky amateur who got lucky. All I needed was a final touch to the scene so even the stupidest investigator would come to the right - from my viewpoint - conclusion.

161

I thought for a moment, then decided that a jealous lover who was unbalanced enough to shoot two people wouldn't waste time in regrets and probably wouldn't be all that rational. He would want to justify his action, at least to himself. Hoping that I wasn't being too clever, I bent over and daubed my forefinger in a puddle of blood. Feeling a little Machiavellian, I carefully drew a large "A" on Frieda's forehead, figuring that at least one person in the local police department would have heard of Hawthorne's *The Scarlet Letter* and draw the obvious conclusion.

I wiped my finger on Krueger's shirt and, gathering up the doctor's notes, walked out into the night and threw up…

It happens like that, and at the time I envied Nick - my ice-cold and now missing classmate - and the fanatical Jacob. They wouldn't be standing there puking their guts out because the mission required the death of an innocent little girl. I had been relieved when she gave me an excuse to shoot her, but I would have in any case; hence the attack of conscience. Well, I could live with it - I hoped - and would consider myself lucky if all I had to worry about was losing my dinner.

A couple of months later - I got back to London using the route I had described to Frieda - I narrowly escaped being blown up by one of the new "V-2" missiles. It gave me a new perspective on the havoc that the German's could have created had they been able to perfect a guidance system. I was told by Mac that our experts agreed that Krueger had been on the right track and, with the papers I had brought back, we should eventually be able to develop our own version of a guided missile, although without a genius like Krueger, it would take years.

That made me feel a little better. I had saved the world from destruction - for the time being - and that made up for the death of one unimportant little girl - didn't it?

Chapter 25

It was some time in late November '44. They brought this big kid up to me on the airfield saying that since I was lone-wolfing it this trip there was plenty of room, and if I didn't mind, it would save their making an extra run. He wasn't one of ours - he was OSS or something - and I wasn't crazy about having any outsiders knowing where I'd been dropped, but there wasn't much I could do about it.

Nobody bothered to introduce us. We didn't have names around that place, anyway; we were just cargo to be delivered. I shook hands with the boy, that was all. He was a knuckle grinder. Then they called that the plane was ready and he wheeled toward it with that same aggressive football readiness of a big man who expects to be hit hard and intends to stay on his feet nevertheless.

We hadn't talked on the way across the Channel. We were just two young guys with different destinations, sharing a taxi for a few blocks, and I was wondering, as always, if this was the night my chute wouldn't open or I'd land in some hot wires and fry to death. He had his own thoughts, of a similar nature, probably. He didn't even wish me good luck when it was time for me to drop, but I didn't hold that against him. We had no sentimental traditions or customs in our organization, but in some outfits, I knew, just as among some hunters, it was considered bad form to wish anybody luck at parting.

"So long, fella," was all he said.

I never have liked people who call me fella, so I just gave him a nod as I went out. The hell with him. If you want to make buddies, join the infantry. The umbrella opened fine, and I landed in an open field, and I never saw the guy again.

The mission involved a prison-break operation at St. Alice. My job was to take the commandant out of action with a scoped-up rifle just before they blew the gates. I got the damn commandant, all right, but nobody else showed up. Well, that wasn't completely unexpected. Mac had warned me of the possibility, when we planned this cockamamie mission in the first place.

I knew I was in trouble when Mac started the meeting with a bone-chilling question. "Eric," he asked, "How high is your pain threshold?"

I paused for a moment, absorbing the implications in the question. "How high does it have to be, Sir?"

He raised his eyebrows a little. They were jet black, in startling contrast to his prematurely gray hair. "Fair enough," he replied. "Let's just say that this mission may require you to endure some unpleasant, but not permanent, damage in order to persuade someone that you are important enough to pass on to his superior for expert interrogation."

Mac speaks English, not gobbledygook. He remembers the nice distinction, almost forgotten nowadays, between convince and persuade. Decimate means, literally, to kill one-tenth of. You can't decimate to the last man - there are always nine left. It may be used loosely to mean inflict large losses upon, but it does not and cannot possibly mean to massacre or annihilate. Disinterested does not mean uninterested and presently means in a little while - not at present and the fact that some permissive dictionaries have already adopted the recent bastard usage doesn't make it sound any less affected and pretentious to his ears or mine.

My mind tends to work like that sometimes. It picks up on the inconsequential while processing the reality on some deeper level. Mac waited patiently. "With all due respect, Sir, damage from 'expert interrogation' is usually more than unpleasant and, more often than not, fairly permanent."

He gave me a reproving look. "It is not in the plan to allow the 'expert interrogation' to take place. You will have a back-up team, comprised of two of our field men, plus an I-Team."

The "I-Team" was a rather specialized group of interrogation experts. I was beginning to get the idea. "You want this superior, I gather?"

"We very much want this superior," he confirmed. "We know *what* he is, but have no idea of who or where he is. Over the last year, it has become clear that someone is training agents and infiltrating them into some of our intelligence and operations units, and at least one fairly important group within the French Resistance."

"... And I'm the bait." It wasn't a question.

"You're the bait," he confirmed. I was a little surprised as Mac often talks around the point. "There are certain elements within the German intelligence community that would dearly love to get their hands on a member of our little group, if for nothing else than to prove to their superiors that we actually exist."

Mac looked at me for a moment, taking my silence as assent. He wasn't much for asking for volunteers. His attitude was that when we volunteered to join the organization, we automatically volunteered for whatever assignment we were given.

"The man's name, at least on his papers, is William Price, known as 'Bill.' He was born in Indianapolis of an American father and a French mother, graduated from Indiana University with an Engineering degree, and volunteered for the Army in 1942. He was commissioned and served with an intelligence unit for two years. Shortly after D-Day, he was assigned as liaison to a unit in the French Resistance. Two months later his unit was ambushed and only he survived, with minor injuries. He eventually made his way to another unit, where he was gratefully accepted.

"Here's what he looks like." He handed me a rather grainy photo, obviously blown up from an official photo ID. "His vitals are on the back. There's no question that a Bill Price with the proper background existed. The only question is whether this is the same

Bill Price who survived the ambush and is now leaking intelligence to the Germans. I guess it would matter to his parents and friends, but to us it makes no difference."

"It's been confirmed that he is, in fact, a spy? Or is that part of my assignment?"

"It has been confirmed sufficiently enough that he may be getting suspicious. I was requested to make him a designated target, until an alternative was proposed." I knew better than to ask whose alternative.

"There's a prison camp outside of a town called St. Alice, with only a small contingent of relatively new and mostly ill-trained guards. Price has been briefed that a 'specialist' has been assigned to take out the Camp Commandant just before he and his Resistance group blow the front gate. They may actually show up."

"May?"

"As I said, he might be getting suspicious. Rather than take the risk of going through with the prison break, he just might decide to blow it off and take you himself, with or without some help."

Chapter 26

My left ear itched. Once early on, as the British say, I went through a door carelessly and got a leg shot out from under me, even though I'd had a feeling something was wrong. So now I respect any little warning tickle. In my line of work, you get these premonitions a hundred times, and ninety-nine times nothing at all happens; but it only takes once.

I rolled to the right several times, ending up on my back with my rifle pointing behind my previous position. Nobody was there. Feeling a little foolish, I started to get up when I heard a rustling sound coming from about 20 or 30 yards into the trees, behind the rocks I had chosen for my vantage point to target the Commandant.

With Mac's warning on my mind, I had arrived at the prison camp hours before the scheduled break, just in case someone was being cute. I'm pretty good in the woods, if I do say so myself, so I had carefully scouted the area and had come to the conclusion that I was alone. I picked a spot between some rocks that gave me a good view into the camp, but shielded me from behind by a couple of boulders and the tree line that started just a few feet behind me. I had several cold hours of boredom ahead of me, but that was pretty much a given for a dedicated hunter. As I was now hunting a different prey, some of whom shot back, I considered a few uncomfortable hours to be a reasonable trade-off for ensuring I didn't get shot in the back.

Apparently, someone had arrived after I had and, rather than try to hunt me down, simply waited for my shots to give away my position. It was kind of rough on the Commandant, but it's the choice I would have made....

Unless this Bill Price was stupid – and the evidence argued strongly against that – he wouldn't try to take me by himself in the middle of a fairly large wooded area. Even two people would have a good chance of missing me altogether. That meant he had at least two others with him, maybe more. I listened carefully and heard the same sound coming from a little to the right of the previous direction. He was circling around my position. Pulling myself up into a crouching position, I headed just to the left of the direction of the rustling sound, intending to get behind him. When they're hunting you, particularly if there are more of them than there are of you, it so seldom occurs to them that you might have the temerity to turn around and come hunting them.

I had to get myself captured by Price, but that didn't mean I had to just sit there, waiting for someone to come up and get the drop on me – or hit me over the head with something. With all the literature on the subject, people had a tendency to overestimate the durability of the human scalp. Not to mention that several good men and women have died, probably amazed and incredulous, at the hands of inexperienced and frightened jerks who'd cut loose when no reasonable person would have dreamed of pulling a trigger. I figured the world could afford to do without one or two of the jerks who picked up guns and went hunting a Helm. Getting mad at a man who has a gun, or lots of men who have lots of guns, is not only stupid, it is dangerous. I have a very primitive reaction. Any time anybody comes after me with a gun, or points a gun at me and tells me to do something he has no right to tell me to do, I find my mind filled with one simple thought: "How do I kill this sonofabitch?"

He really wasn't very good in the woods. Once I got within 50 feet of him, I could him track by the racket he was making. He didn't know where to walk and apparently just assumed that small branches would bend out of his way rather than breaking with a sharp cracking sound. After a few minutes, he got tired of circling and made a right-angle turn toward my original position. Either he thought I might be stupid enough to stay in place or he had some wild notion that he could track me from there. I cut across the diagonal to intercept him at the tree line beside my sniper nest. With the noise he was making, he probably couldn't have heard me coming if I broke into a sprint, but I walked carefully anyway, although a little faster than he was moving.

168

A few minutes later, squatting behind some brush behind a tree, I saw him coming through the trees. It wasn't Price. He was in uniform and carrying some kind of machine pistol. He stopped for a moment and looked around at the rocks, perhaps hoping to find me still lying down watching the prison yard. He slowly walked past my position, still looking for me. Suspecting nothing from the rear, he was taken completely by surprise when, as he passed in front of my tree, I put down my rifle, rose up and threw the lock on him from behind. He was little over six feet tall, outweighed me by a good 30 pounds, so he was too big for me to mess with. I gave it maximum effort instantly, therefore, and felt certain important items break in certain important places. I held him like that until there were no more kicks or quivers or spasmodic tremors left in him, and even a little longer. Too many good men have died - well, they thought they were good - because they were too sensitive, spelled queasy, to make absolutely certain. There was little noise, just the scuffle of feet, some heavy breathing - mostly mine, since my grip hadn't let him have much air - and a small scraping sound as I dragged him out of sight.

I should have paid more attention to that left ear. As I straightened up, I felt something hard jab into my spine. With a bit of admiration, I realized what he had done. He'd sent his city-bred companion into the woods after me, hoping I'd take the bait, while he'd waited for me to show myself. Not knowing where I'd end up, he had to have followed me, which spoke well for his woodsman skills. Of course, with all the noise his partner had been making, he probably could have stayed five feet behind me and I wouldn't have heard him.

I stood absolutely still, waiting for his next move. Sticking a gun barrel into a professional's back is not the brightest idea in the world. There are a couple of basic moves that can result in the gunman's immediate disability, not to say death. With the gun barrel pressed hard against one's back, a quick turn will move the gun away from the body, leaving the gunman off balance and exposed to instant mayhem. Since the idea was to get captured, I restrained my natural impulse. Even so, he must have seen my involuntary muscle-tightening in preparation for the automatic

169

move I had had drummed into my head back in training, as he moved back a step, relieving the pressure on my spine.

"Careful, Eric," he said. "It is Eric, isn't it?"

"Yes, and you're Price."

He gave a short laugh. "Bill Price at your service. The man you were sent to kill."

Mac had been right about Price's suspicions. That was why he had cancelled his group's participation in the prison break. Since I was scheduled to meet up with his group for their help with my escape route after the assignment was completed, he couldn't take the risk of going through with it. Thinking his cover was blown anyway, he had apparently decided to do exactly what Mac had hoped – take me alive to salvage something from his efforts. At least, it appeared that was what he had in mind as, if he had intended to kill me, he could have done so at any time in the last few minutes. His assumption that I had a secondary mission to kill him hadn't really been considered by Mac – or me – but from my perspective, it seemed an idea worth encouraging.

"Yeah, I was kind of hoping that was you making all the racket."

"Fortunately for me, I'm pretty good in the woods. Helmut – that's the name of the soldier laying there – wasn't very good at all, which was why I sent him after you first. Nice job, by the way." He sounded genuinely sincere. Then he raised his voice a little. "Hans! Josef! Hier!" Well, I'd thought there were at least three of them. Apparently, there were four … or had been.

"Put your hands behind your head, Eric, and turn around slowly. Do you have any other weapons, other than that rifle over there?" He was watching my eyes as he asked. I could play that game, too.

"Just a small folding knife in my pocket, not much good for anything but paring my fingernails," I replied, with no hesitation. After Mac's training, I could lie with the best of them. Taped

170

between my shoulders, it was an interesting little rig - a flat little sheath holding a flat little knife with a kind of pear-shaped symmetrical blade and a couple of thin pieces of fiber-board riveted on to form a crude handle. The point and edges were honed, but not very sharp because you don't make throwing knives of highly tempered steel unless you want them to shatter on impact. It wouldn't be much of a weapon - a quick man could duck it and a heavy coat would stop it - but it would be right there when someone pointed a gun at you and ordered you to raise your hands or, even better, clasp them at the back of your neck. Slide a hand down inside the neckline of your shirt or blouse and you were armed again. And there can be situations when even as little as five inches of not very sharp steel flickering through the air can make all the difference in the world.

I forced my mind away from the knife. I've found that, sometimes, if you think too much about something, someone else starts thinking about it too. I know, that sounds about as silly as my left ear itching for a warning, but you live your life your way and I'll live mine my way. Anyway, I was here to get captured by the guy, not toss a knife into his throat….

The rustling sounds behind Price told me Hans and Josef were on their way. Price's grimace told me he heard them as well. "What can you do with these people brought up in the city? It's a wonder they even found us. Are you a hunter, Eric? You move like one."

"I've done some hunting in my time, although I'm used to animals that are a little harder to track than your friend Helmut over there."

He laughed. "No hard feelings, Eric. I'd have done the same, although, I must admit, not quite as efficiently." He looked at me sharply. "But then, I didn't have the specialized training you did."

He was guessing, trying to put the pieces together. The problem he had was trying to convince his superiors that Americans could be as ruthless and cold-blooded as the "Master Race."

When I didn't reply, he had Josef search me. Josef was quite thorough and managed to find the knife in my pocket, overlooking the one taped to my back, and not even checking my boots to see if I had a small pistol or a knife tucked down the top of one or both of them. Price looked at me at raised his eyebrows in an expression that said, "What can you do?" and told Josef to check my boots.

Price jerked his head to the side. "Let's get going. Sooner or later those kids in the prison are going to get the idea that nothing else is going to happen and come out looking for the sniper who shot their Commandant. Eric, you keep at least 15 feet behind me."

We headed off through the woods with Price leading the way and Hans and Josef following me off to the side and a little behind so if they had to shoot me, nobody else would be in the line of fire. They weren't much in the woods but, otherwise, appeared to be fairly professional. Eventually we came to a black sedan. Opening the trunk, Price produced a length of rope and proceeded to tie my hands together in front of me. He had me get in the back with Josef, and Hans took the passenger seat in front of me. About an hour later, we parked in front of a small cabin. Leaving the two soldiers to stand guard, Price motioned me into the cabin, followed me in and shut the door behind us.

It was small, with a kitchen off to one side and a bedroom off to the other. I could see a small portable propane stove just inside the kitchen, and a wood-burning heater against the long wall of the living room. Apparently, in anticipation of capturing me alive, the stove had been on and it was comfortable in the cabin. Price removed his coat, threw it on the short couch and indicated that I should do the same.

"Ok, Eric, it's time we talked. Who do you work for?"

I looked at him and laughed. "For *whom* do you *want* me to work?"

Chapter 27

He flushed and backhanded me across the face. Getting no answer to his question, he took another swing at me. The forehand wasn't as bad as the backhand since I didn't get the knuckles or the stones of the rings he was wearing, but I made it look spectacular, flinching away from the blow and letting myself lose my balance and go down. They always enjoy knocking you down; and when they're beating on you, you want to keep them happy. If you make them sad, they may actually hurt you.

I felt a little blood running from my nose; I made no effort to sniff it back. They love the sight of blood - other folks' blood - and the human body holds several quarts. I could spare a few drops for public relations. He stepped forward and kicked me in the side as I crouched there in abject terror for a minute or so. Then I sat up defiantly and made the appropriate responses, commenting on his parentage. You can cut any similar dialogue from a movie and fit it in here - they expect it. It all sounds pretty corny to me, but he found it convincing enough to give me a backhand crack to the side of the face. One of his rings nicked me above the right eyebrow and produced a little more blood for his pleasure.

I was concerned with the timing: Could I yield convincingly now or should I wait until I had a few more cuts and bruises and he brought out the knife he was bound to produce. I mean, I'd been here before. The moves are predictable. Reluctantly deciding that I couldn't give in too easily, I kept my mouth shut and waited for his next move.

Price walked to the door and told Josef to bring some more rope. When Josef came in carrying a coil of rope, Price asked him for my knife – surprise! - and told him to keep me covered. He walked over to the small stove just inside the kitchen, making sure I could see what he was doing, and turned on one of the two gas burners. He opened the knife and set it beside the burner with the blade over the flame. Reaching behind him, he grabbed a kitchen chair and set it in the middle of the living room next to me.

"Sit in the chair, Eric," he ordered. I hesitated and, as he drew back his foot for another kick, slowly got up off the floor and sat in the chair. Being careful not to get in Josef's way, he untied my hands and retied them behind the back of the chair, securing them to the chair. He then tied my legs to the front legs of the chair and motioned Josef back outside.

Reaching toward me with both hands, he slowly unbuttoned my shirt, smiling at me. He then walked over and took his gloves out of his coat pocket and put on the right-hand glove. He went to the kitchen and retrieved my knife, grabbing the handle in his gloved right hand....

It was like a lot of physical tortures - it's rough, but pain is pain. I mean, it's worse than hitting your thumb with a heavy hammer or dropping a brick on your toe because it didn't stop. It's about like having a clumsy, persistent dentist working on you without Novocain. People have stood that and I stood this, but I don't pretend I was heroic about it. I grunted and sweated as it went on; I even considered screaming occasionally but decided against it. Things were tough enough without adding a gag to my discomforts. Hate and thoughts of revenge are usually the way to get through it. You concentrate on the torturer as someone you are going to kill very slowly, very deliberately, very painfully when *your* time comes. The ingenious torments you devise for him - or her - keep you going during the times when the disinterested-spectator technique doesn't quite work any more.

You don't have to bluster about it, but you can think about it: you concentrate on visualizing the scene when it is your turn. First you work it out with a gun: smash the knee and elbow joints, shoot the fingers off one by one, blast the eardrums with the muzzle held close, and blow away the testicles. One thing you don't want to do is blind the bastard. You want him to be able to watch you enjoying yourself. You want him to see and appreciate what's happening to him. You want him to know he played his tic-tac-toe

174

on the wrong guy's chest and got himself totally ruined; and then maybe you can afford to be nice and put one between the eyes to end it. Or maybe not. Okay. So what about a knife, let's figure it with a knife. A knife is always good, and you can perform more delicately painful operations with a blade that you can with a bullet.... Oh, Jesus, how long is the sonofabitch going to keep this up, anyway?

He aimed the knife at my left eye. "You can stop it anytime, Eric," he taunted. I hesitated, a man struggling toward a reluctant decision. I shook my head and said, "Okay! Enough, dammit!"

He looked at me for a moment and then nodded. He walked into the kitchen and came back with a glass of water. Holding it to my lips, he let me drain most of it.

"Okay, Eric, for *whom* do you work?"

"… There's a man called Mac. I report to him. We really don't have an official name, although we refer to ourselves as the M-Group…."

This went on for a while, me spinning the half-truths, real truths and complete fiction Mac and I had concocted, and Price interrupting with questions and occasional threats with the knife. I gave him enough information for him to convince himself he had the real goods and enough evasion and "I don't knows" that he was sure I knew more than I was willing to tell him.

I knew I had him hooked when he said, "We're going to take a little trip, Eric. There is someone who will really want to meet you."

He went into the kitchen and came back with a first-aid kit. Taking off the glove, he rummaged in the kit and came up with a small tube of some kind of ointment. "This may help a little," he said, as he smeared the gunk over the cuts and burns on my chest.

A half-hour later, with my bladder emptied, my shirt buttoned up and my coat on, I was securely tied hand-and-foot, placed in the front seat of the car, and tied to the seat support so I couldn't reach Price or open the door and throw myself out. This was encouraging, as it indicated that we were going to lose Hans and Josef somewhere along the way. I hoped my back-up team was doing their job....

Chapter 28

About an hour later, we entered a medium-sized town, turned off the main road and, a few blocks down, parked in front of a small brick house. Price went into the house, along with Hans and Josef, and came back out alone, carrying two opened bottles of beer. He opened the passenger door and held one bottle to my lips, letting me take a long swallow. "Enjoy it, Eric," he said. "You'll forgive me if I don't untie your hands and let you hold the bottle."

I've never been a great beer fan, but this one tasted about as good as anything I've ever had. Thirst, stress and a physical beating will do that to you. He let me finish the bottle, threw it in the yard, closed my door and went around to the driver's side and off we went again.

"Let me guess," I ventured. "We're going somewhere Hans and Josef have no business knowing about."

"Correct, Eric," Price replied. With a hint of pride in his voice, he continued, "Only four of us even know of Doktor Vogelmann's presence here in France. He will be very interested in talking with you."

"Vogelmann," I repeated, more to myself than to Price. "The name sounds familiar ..." Then a name popped up from a briefing a couple of months before. "Wait a minute, wasn't he a protégé of Otto Skorzeny?"

Price looked over at me sharply. "What do you know of General Skorzeny, Eric?"

I immediately regretted my outburst. Our knowledge of Skorzeny was a little bit more information than I should have given him. Covering up, I replied, "Not all that much. He was supposed to be some kind of spymaster before he got promoted. I just remembered hearing of a civilian English professor joining his staff – a Doktor Vogelmann, educated in the U.S. and later joining the faculty of Frankfurt University in the late 30s. We tend to keep track of German nationals educated in the U.S., especially when they associate with high-ranking German officials."

He relaxed a little. "You have a very good memory. Yes, that is the same Doktor Vogelmann. His backgound has been very valuable to General Skorzeny."

I let that pass and we drove in silence for the next hour or so. I must have dozed off for a while, in spite of the dull ache on my chest, because I awoke with a start as the car came to a halt. I looked up and saw a small cottage surrounded by trees, with a black Mercedes parked in front of us. Looking to the sides, I couldn't see any neighbors, just more trees on one side and a rolling hill on the other.

"We're here, Eric," Price explained. Then, with a look of admiration, he asked, "How can you sleep?"

"I learned a long time ago not to worry too much about things I can't control. Besides, in my business, I never know when I'll get a chance to sleep, so I take it when I can."

"A good philosophy. I will have to practice that."

He got out and came around to my side. He untied my feet and untied me from the seat support, leaving my hands tied. "Come on, Eric, let's go meet Doktor Vogelmann."

As I got out of the car, I looked back away from the house. The driveway in which we had parked intersected a road at right angles. Looking down the road in both directions, I could see turns that would hide the approach of my back-up team, assuming they were still with us.

I sincerely hoped they were parked somewhere just out of sight and didn't take all night, because if they didn't show, I was going to find out once and for all what was on the other side of that fabled "bright light." Hidden in my clothing – never mind where – was a little "kill me" pill which I could reach so long as my hands remained tied in front. All field agents carry one; when it was issued, we were told it was fairly unpleasant but quick….

I turned toward the house and walked to the front door, Price following me. Vogelmann was obviously expecting us and opened the door while we were still halfway there. I'm not sure what I was expecting – perhaps some fictionalized evil genius with burning eyes and a sneering expression. What I got was a fiftyish, balding gray-haired professor, medium build with the standard wire-rimmed eyeglasses. He had a pleasant face, a weak chin and a charming smile … until you saw his eyes. They weren't smiling at all.

He stood back to let us in, staying a few feet from me once he saw my hands were tied in front. Once we were inside, he closed the door and turned to Price first. "Good work, Herr Price," he said. Price smiled and made a slight bow.

Turning to me, he said, "Welcome … Eric, isn't it? My name, if Bill hasn't already told you, is Heinrich Vogelmann."

I nodded my head, saying, "Happy to meet you Doktor." I held up my hands. "You'll forgive me for not shaking your hand, but …"

"Ah, yes. I'm afraid I will just have to forgo the pleasure, Eric. According to Bill, here, it might not be wise to untie you." Again, I got the charming smile. It was quite an asset for a spy.

Vogelmann waved his hand toward an overstuffed couch. "If you and Bill will sit there …" I sat on one end and Price sat on the other, keeping his gun trained on me. He continued, "Would you care for a drink? I've got some beer and a fairly good chilled Riesling."

I opted for the Riesling while Price stuck with beer. Vogelmann came back shortly with Price's beer in a bottle, his own wine in a crystal wine glass and my wine in a light metal cup. I just grinned at him as I took the cup in my hands. It's nice to be respected even when tied up.

He sat in a chair located on my side of the couch at a right angle to it, and took a sip of his wine. "Now, Mr. Helm, suppose you recap for me the story your told Herr Price." I raised my eyebrows. Our code names were not really considered a secret, merely an identification device to keep our real names secret. "Eric" was known to quite a lot of people by now; however, my real name was known only to a select few. Hell, most of Mac's people didn't know it, let alone some German spymaster.

"Surprised?" Vogelmann smiled. "We have heard several stories over the years of a tall, blond, rather lanky gentleman who has been variously described as American, German, French or Scandinavian. Regardless of the nationality, all these stories had one thing in common. Wherever this man was seen, dead bodies inevitably were left behind.

"A few months ago, one of our agents sent back some information about a young American officer, tall, blond, very proficient with weapons and his hands, who seemed to have disappeared from an officers' training camp and was subsequently spotted using the name 'Eric.' It was suspected that he was working for some kind of intelligence organization that specialized in various forms of mayhem one would not think would be countenanced by the tender American psyche. You have been quite active, Eric, and have drawn a lot of interest in some quarters."

There didn't seem to be anything to say to that, so I just sat there, digesting all this.

Before he could continue, there was the sound of a truck of some kind passing in front of the house, followed by a loud backfire a few seconds later, as the driver changed gears clumsily. Nobody paid much attention other than to look instinctively toward the general direction from which it had come. I mean, it's only in the movies or novels that a backfire sounds much like anything else but a backfire. It especially doesn't sound like a gunshot. I was very carefully not paying attention to it as I had been expecting it. Well, not specifically a backfire, but any one of several signals my backup team would use, depending upon the circumstances. It meant that I had about five minutes to do something, get out of the way or, as the present situation indicated, just sit still until it was time to dive for cover. My main concern was the pistol Price was holding in his hand, still in my general direction. That could create a problem.

With only a short pause, Vogelmann continued. "The reason I am telling you this, Eric, is that when you repeat the story you told Herr Price, you might reconsider any, shall we say, flights of fancy?"

That upset Price, who protested, "I broke him, Doktor Vogelmann. He wasn't lying. He wouldn't risk any more pain."

Vogelmann held up his hand. "Bill, I'm not doubting your expertise, but we both know people will say a lot of things they think you want to hear in order to avoid pain. I just want to separate the truth from the fiction … well, as much as we can here with my limited resources. In Germany, we can do a much better job of … debriefing." This time his smile was not so charming.

"Well, Eric? Or should I let Herr Price pick up where he left off?"

It seemed like a good idea to keep them occupied concentrating on me, so I related the story again, adding in a couple of details I hadn't told Price. Vogelmann asked a couple of questions but, for the most part, appeared content to just let me talk, nodding now and then. It didn't take long – just long enough. I was trying to think of something else to say when we heard a back window break.

Both of them jumped up and turned toward the bedroom, Price taking both his gun and his eyes off of me. He managed about two steps toward the bedroom before the front door smashed in and two of the most beautiful sights in my life came rushing through the opening, each carrying a machine gun. They were good. They had orders to take Vogelmann alive and Price was right in the line of fire, so they held their fire and split in opposite directions, looking for a clean shot.

By that time I had already swung my hands over my head and down the back of my shirt and had my little throwing knife by the hilt. Price started to swing his pistol toward the one on his left, which put the back of his head toward me. Swinging both hands forward, I aimed the knife and let go in a smooth, steady motion. The little knife was beautifully balanced and made one full turn before imbedding itself in the soft spot on the back of Price's neck, just below the skull. He continued to turn but it was just momentum at that point – he was dead on his feet. He made a little spiral and fell flat on his face.

I looked to the side and saw one of my backup team covering Vogelmann with his gun. I didn't recognize him, but I knew the other one. We had been on two missions together. He was still covering Price, just in case. Like I said, they were good. I got up and went over to him and held my hands out. He pulled a knife from a belt sheath with one hand and cut the rope, freeing my hands. "Thanks, Rusty," I said. "Who's your partner?"

"That's Evan. We got him a few months ago."

I walked over to Price and kicked him over on his back. Then I bent down and reached into his right-hand pants pocket.

"What the hell are you doing, Eric?" That came from Evan. I pulled out my hand and showed him the Solingen knife. "The sonofabitch took my knife and I'm kind of attached to it." He nodded as though it was perfectly natural for me to be thinking of my knife right after killing a man. Hell, it was. Back at base I had my little Colt Woodsman .22 waiting for me. We all have our little attachments and superstitions.

"What now?" I asked.

Rusty asked, "What kind of shape are you in?"

"I'm OK, just a few cuts and burns. Nothing permanent."

"Good, you ride in the van with the I-Team and keep an eye on our friend here, while Evan and I follow in our cars. We don't want to leave one around here." I nodded. Any professional shadow job requires multiple vehicles; even an unsuspecting target can get suspicious if he sees the same car behind him for miles.

Rusty continued, "We don't know how much time we have before someone comes looking for ..."

"His name is Heinrich Vogelman."

He arched his eyebrows. "Ah. That figures." He had been at the briefing, too. "Anyway, we'll take the body and both their cars and ditch them so if anybody comes sniffing around, they'll just think Vogelmann is out ... we hope." He handed me his weapon. "Here, you watch Vogelmann while Evan and I clean up and get a couple members of the I-Team to drive their cars."

About 45 minutes later, we found a dirt road running into a mini-forest and turned onto it. While driving, I had Vogelmann sitting on a bench seat on one side of the van while I sat across from him, holding the gun on him. The other two I-Team members were up front, one driving and the other in the passenger seat. They had shaken my hand and introduced themselves, but hadn't said anything else. As far as I knew we had two I-Teams in our little group and both had four members. I never asked why.

All around us were interesting pieces of equipment, most of which I didn't recognize. Some of them, however, were very recognizable, which probably accounted for the beads of sweat on Vogelmann's forehead and the darkening stains at his armpits. He hadn't said a word since Rusty and Evan had broken into his house.

Finally, we stopped. A couple of minutes later, the back door on the van opened and the other two I-Team members motioned me out and climbed into the van. Rusty and Evan were waiting outside.

Rusty looked a little uncomfortable. "Eric, I have a request from Mac for you. He said he would understand if you declined, but he would like for you to watch the I-Team at work. He said the knowledge might come in handy some day."

I paused for a moment and then, to buy a little more time I asked if he had witnessed an interrogation. "No," he replied. "I was given a chance once, but decided not to, but that was an I-Team member asking, not Mac."

And, of course, that was the crux. I nodded. "Ok, I'm in. Where are we going?"

Rusty grinned. "Right here, right now. We don't know how long we've got before someone finds Vogelmann missing. Hell, he might have called someone while you were on the way to his house and they're on the way now. We've got to get the information on the moles before they're alerted."

"What about you and Evan?

"Evan is going to report in by radio from a safe house we have access to about 40 miles away. I'll stay here until they're finished and drive us to meet Evan and relay the information."

"What happens if they can't break him?"

"They will. Trust me."

They did. I had to leave twice to throw up and I still have nightmares…

Chapter 29

There were a lot of people - actually, most - in Mac's outfit I didn't know; and while we were vaguely aware that the British had at least one group that approximated ours, I had not been formally introduced to one before. We didn't have cozy get-acquainted office parties, quite the contrary. Mac operates on the principle that the fewer of your colleagues you've met, the fewer you can betray if somebody starts asking the rough way.

It was, therefore, surprising that I knew only one guy in the group assembled in Mac's briefing room. What was more surprising was just how many – eight in all – I *didn't* know. Being one of his senior operatives by then, simply by virtue of survival, I knew quite a few more of Mac's people than most, and had worked with many of them several times. In line with his philosophy, when teams were needed on a field operation, Mac tended to use people who already knew one another rather than unnecessarily exposing too much information about another agent, unless the agent had talents necessary to the operation.

I glanced over at Martinson, who responded by raising his eyebrows and giving a slight shrug of his shoulders. Martinson had already been working for Mac when I first arrived and we had been on two missions together. He was, perhaps, the deadliest fighter I had ever known, myself definitely not excepted. Give him a rifle, a pistol, a knife, a garrote, or no weapon but his hands and feet, and his opponent was dead. Off duty, he had a wide-ranging sense of humor and enjoyed practical jokes, which seemed a little odd, given his single-minded pursuit of mayhem in the field. In any organization like ours, legends grow about the senior operatives who managed to survive, passed along in whispers to the new boys - Fedder and Rasmussen, who almost always worked as a team, Barnett, who moved like a ghost … and Martinson, who was rumored to have personally killed over three dozen targets, not counting collateral damage.

Martinson's presence – and my own, to flatter myself a bit – among such a large group of unknowns being briefed by Mac personally, signaled a wide departure from our usual *modus operandi*. Usually, in a large operation, two or three agents were briefed on the objective, allowed to formulate their own tactics, and either hand-picked or were assigned the rest of the team who were brought up to speed individually. This had the feel of a fully-planned operation, and I started to get a sinking feeling in the pit of my stomach. I just hoped it was Mac's plan and not one passed on by the group of geniuses who had ignored all the signals of the impending *Unternehmen Wacht am Rhein* the previous December, which had come close to giving Hitler a reprieve from the seemingly inevitable defeat of Germany. Apparently, intelligence reports, some supplied by one of Mac's people, second hand, had been largely ignored. Translated as Operation "The Guard on the Rhine" or Operation "Watch on the Rhine," depending upon your translation preferences, it became known to the public as "The Battle of the Bulge." Taken by surprise, the allies put up little resistance at first and the offensive nearly succeeded. Only extraordinary heroism and a refusal to quit on the part of an amazingly large number of troops, both British and American, had eventually turned back the advance. It cost us over 70,000 casualties, but Germany suffered even more.

My reverie was interrupted by Mac's entrance. Carrying a briefcase, he strode up to the lectern and turned to face us, setting the briefcase down beside him. I couldn't tell anything from his expression, but then, I never could. Ignoring the briefcase, he started speaking to us. "Good morning, gentlemen," he said, "Welcome to Operation Silver Bullet. I'm not going to make any introductions, as those of you who will need to know each other already do, and the less the rest of you know, the better. For purposes of identification, you will be known as 'Blue Two'" – he pointed to a blond guy on his far left – "'Blue Three', 'Blue Four' ..." He continued in order until all of us had been given a designation. I was "Blue Eight" and Martinson was "Blue Five."

After the last "Blue" had been named, he continued, "You will meet Blue One once the operation has begun. Memorize the name and face of each member here. You will need to know both later. Other than that, all you need to know is that several different organizations are represented here, never mind which organization or who belongs to which."

He paused a moment as we each looked around at the others, putting the names and faces together as we had all undoubtedly been trained to do. I mean, "Recognition 101" or whatever you choose to call it is pretty standard fare for any intelligence organization, even a specialized unit like ours. My stomach was not soothed by the revelation that the group included "several different organizations." I often had enough trouble putting up with the prima donnas that Mac had trained, let alone some unknown spymaster.

"OK," Mac continued, "Some background first. Has anyone here ever heard of Otto Skorzeny?"

A couple of hands went up. Mac nodded at Blue Nine, who asked, "Isn't he the guy on all those 'wanted' posters Eisenhower papered Allied territory with?"

"Yes, that is he." There were a few nods around the room. "Part of his mission was to create confusion and spread disinformation during the recent German offensive, using hand-picked German soldiers who could pass for Americans. His people had instructions, if captured, to tell their interrogators that Skorzeny's mission was a raid on Paris to kill or capture General Eisenhower. It worked and, evidently, General Eisenhower was not amused by spending Christmas in a security lockdown."

He waited for a moment as the inevitable smiles appeared on some faces, including mine. I had heard the rumors too. Mac continued, "General Skorzeny has been very valuable to the Fatherland in many different capacities; however, only one of those is of concern to us here and it is related to the Eisenhower incident. A couple of years ago, Skorzeny came up with the idea of recruiting and training German soldiers to pass as Americans. His goal was not espionage, but sabotage, spreading disinformation and generally creating havoc among the Allied troops, usually in support of German operations."

Blue Three, obviously from another organization, interrupted, "So Skorzeny is our target?"

Mac frowned. He liked getting to the point in his own time and wasn't fond of interruptions, something we all learned early on. Apparently, Mac was in a cooperative mood, so he didn't fry the guy. "No, Skorzeny has been promoted to bigger and better things; however, the training of American imposters continues … with a twist.

"As the defeat of Germany became more and more inevitable, the purpose of the training was changed to dealing with the eventual occupation by the Allies. As envisioned by Himmler, it was to become a stay-behind Nazi organization, which would engage in guerrilla warfare against the occupying troops. However, the Nazi generals, including Skorzeny, soon realized that the groups of recruits were too few in number to be an effective fighting force. It has now been decided to use them to set up systems of escape routes, called 'Ratlines'" – Mac pronounced it correctly as "rattlins." The word comes from a nautical term for lines used to form a rope ladder – "a sort of secret 'underground railroad' to help leading Nazis escape after Germany's surrender. These escape routes are intended mainly to lead to safe havens in South America, particularly Argentina, Paraguay, Brazil and Chile; however, there are hints that other destinations may include the United States, Canada and the Middle East."

From the expressions around the room, this was news to everybody. I wanted to ask where all this inside information came from, but I knew Mac too well; he would either tell us in time or simply fall back on the old "need to know" axiom.

"The organization," Mac continued, "which is now calling the shots is called 'Organisation der ehemaligen SS-Angehörigen,' or *ODESSA* for short." I assumed we all spoke German because Mac didn't volunteer the English translation: "The Organization of

Former SS-Members." I guessed things must be pretty grim in Berlin when new secret organizations were already using "former" in their descriptions.

"Himmler's designation for these highly-specialized agents of Skorzeny's training course was *Werwolfs*." Nobody needed a translation for that one. "Most of the new crop of *Werwolfs* are relatively inexperienced, since the main requirements are having an extensive knowledge of America and the ability to speak American English fluently. Although they are given training in sabotage, demolitions, small arms, survival and radio-communications, their success will be largely dependent upon leadership from a small group of experienced officers, hand-picked from the ranks of the German Army and the Waffen SS. In two weeks, most of these officers will meet at *Schloss Hülchrath*; a castle near the Rhinish town of Erkelenz, to plan their final strategy before disbursing throughout Germany. Our objective is to eliminate as many of these *Werwolfs* leaders as possible, especially their Commandant, one Colonel Franz Weiss."

Chapter 30

Fortunately, the Mercedes-Benz L4500A cargo truck had been fitted with a canopy. The "A" designation appended to the truck model indicated a four-wheel-drive and, in the sloppy and rutted piss-poor excuse for a road we were following, that drive was necessary. Having a cloud cover with a steady drizzle was all well and good for a parachute drop in enemy territory, but driving for hours exposed to the cold and rain would not have put me in the proper frame of mind to start a dangerous mission. I don't like cold, which is a hell of an attitude for a Scandinavian kid born in the cold Northern part of the U.S., but we'd moved to New Mexico – Santa Fe, if it matters - when I was a kid, and I preferred relatively warm, dry climates.

The drop had gone off without a hitch. The pilot had managed to get all 10 of us landed within a mile of the rendezvous point, no mean feat. We had all been equipped with narrow-band, short-range radios and had quickly found our way to the truck. The driver was Blue One, our missing 11th member. According to the insignia on his uniform, he was an SS Captain. During our briefing, Mac had explained that he actually *was* an SS Captain – and a deep cover American agent who had spent four years working himself up through the ranks. He had been responsible for providing the Allies with a lot of valuable information, including some tidbits regarding a top-secret code used by the German Enigma Machine. A few months earlier, he had been recruited as one of the leaders of the *Werwolfs*, and was not only the source of most of our intelligence regarding the group, but was the key to the entire operation – he was our ticket into *Schloss Hülchrath*.

In the back of the truck, Blue One had provided us with an assortment of weapons, including MP38s, grenades, knives and garrotes; various uniforms; and, best of all, several blankets. I was beginning to like this guy. Once we had changed into the dry uniforms – apparently, some of us had been picked for the mission based upon size – Blue Three, our designated expert with the Mercedes cargo truck, got into the driver's seat while Blue One got in back with the rest of us, after opening the back window of the cab to provide us with a little heat as well as allowing Blue Three to listen in on the two-way briefing. We introduced ourselves by our code names.

Mac had briefed us on the overall plan and most of the details, but Blue One hadn't been there, so Blue Two had been appointed to bring him up-to-date...

Mac had opened his briefcase, pulled out 11 folders, passed out one to each of us, and returned to the lectern with his copy. "Gentlemen," he began, "The first page is a diagram of the layout of *Schloss Hülchrath*, courtesy of Blue One. It's a little crude, but he will update you when you see him in Germany. You'll be in a truck and enter at the South across the drawbridge. Yes, there's a drawbridge. It no longer is able to be raised, but it's still the only entrance into the castle. There'll be a checkpoint with a barrier and two soldiers in a shed, more to keep out sightseers and the curious than anything else. Blue One will get you past them with no problem, so leave them alone. You probably can't neutralize them without gunfire and we can't take any chances of alerting the rest of the castle's occupants.

"We don't expect any trainees to be present during the meeting – Blue One wasn't clear on whether the compound is in between training classes, or any trainees were just given the weekend off – so we will ignore the complex on the West side of the grounds for the purposes of this operation. That complex is a replica of part of the downtown area of a small Kansas town called Kingman. The original is located a few miles West of Wichita. There's a movie theater, a drugstore, a hardware store, a grocery store and a couple of other businesses, all of which are normally manned with people who are completely conversant in American slang and culture. The idea is total immersion in anything and everything American for the duration of the training."

There were a few exclamations and hissings of breath around the room as the scope of the Skorzeny's brainchild became evident. In our business, passing for a German was a necessary part of many of our operations, but only for short periods with limited contact. Skorzeny's graduates could wreak havoc with any occupying forces, especially in the chaos following the fall of the German government.

"Exactly," Mac responded to the unspoken, but evident sentiments. "We don't know how many of these fake Americans there are or where they are, and have no idea *who* they are. Our only hope is to disrupt their command structure to the point that they become largely ineffectual, other than on an individual basis.

"As the trainees won't be in residence, we will also ignore these barracks on the East and South sides. This brings us to the castle proper, located toward the North. If you will all turn to the second page, you will see a drawing of the castle itself. Here's an enlarged view." He turned to an easel beside the lectern and flipped a page over the top, revealing the larger drawing of the castle. Picking up a pointer from the tray, he started pointing out rooms. "This large area in the front was designed for entertainment purposes, sort of a massive ballroom. As you'll be arriving late at night, it should be empty except for a soldier or two, who will be expecting you. That should make it easy to take them out … silently, of course. Since we will have no idea exactly where they'll be or which of you will be closest to them, whoever has the opportunity will accomplish that task."

He looked around and was apparently satisfied with the reactions he saw. Well, the squeamish didn't really get very far in our business. He continued, "Back here are the bedrooms, currently set up for four to a room. There are eight bedrooms scattered along these two corridors. There are supposed to be between 25 and 30 guests, not counting the Commandant; however, you 10 will be replacing 10 of the guests, with Blue One's help, leaving you with 15 to 20 targets. We have no idea of the sleeping assignments – perhaps Blue One will be able to provide more information – so anywhere from five to all eight bedrooms may be

192

occupied. Of course, we're hoping that all the guests will be in bed at that hour." I thought I saw a small smile cross Mac's face, but I could have been mistaken.

"Over here, to the West of the castle, is the Commandant's quarters. Colonel Weiss is not fond of sharing a bedroom, so he makes his home in the large guest house. He will have two of his personal guards with him in the house, awake, plus another two or three, depending upon how many are waiting for you in the castle, in the smaller guest house, sleeping during their off shift. Blue Five, Blue Eleven and Blue Eight, you are assigned to take out the Commandant, after disposing of the four or five guards. The rest of you will clear out the bedrooms and anyplace else that might have insomniacs wandering around. Once you have cleared the castle, assist Blue Five and Blue Eight, if necessary, then take care of the two guards you left at the drawbridge.

"Your folders have papers and IDs which should get you through any checkpoints on your way back to France, along with directions, routes, and alternatives in case the primary escape route is compromised or you get separated for any reason. You will all meet at the airport at 1:00 AM the morning of Friday the 26th for your flight and parachute drop to the rendezvous with Blue One. Until then, you've all got a two-week vacation. Any questions?"

I had about a dozen or more and, most likely, so did everybody else, but no one spoke up. Mac had that effect on people.

Once Blue Two had finished, Blue One nodded. "It sounds good," he said. "Now here's the plan for handling the 10 *Werwolfs* you'll be replacing....

Chapter 31

We picked up the first two *Werwolfs* in a mid-size town called Liege. It was almost too easy. They climbed into the back of the truck and were each grabbed by two "Blues" while a third used a garrote. The air got a little thick with an ugly smell from the men at our feet. The sphincters had let go as they often do. Carting dead bodies around isn't quite the nice clean fun they make it seem in certain jolly murder mysteries, literary and cinematic. Thirty minutes outside of the town, we carried their bodies into a small grove of trees and left them there, after transferring the insignia and their papers from their uniforms to two of ours. Two hours later, we did the same to three more in Aachen. That left five in Erkelenz.

We pulled into Erkelenz a little before midnight. The weather was beginning to clear by then, but with the dissipation of the cloud cover, the temperature was dropping. What little heat that was coming through the back window of the cab wasn't helping much. Well, I'd spent colder and more miserable nights in my life, but five dead men behind us and many more soon-to-be-dead ahead of us seemed to just make it colder. The looks on some of the others' faces told me they weren't too comfortable with up-close-and-personal cold-blooded murder either. That's the hard part for some in this business – you can't always just pull a trigger from 300 yards away and watch someone fall down. I guessed Mac had carefully chosen who would do the holding and who would do the garroting. Martinson had handled two of them.

We parked at the side of a building with a sign proclaiming it to be the *Wegberg Gasthaus. Gasthaus* translates as 'Inn.' Blue One had decided it was too risky trying to handle all five of them at once, so the plan was for him to go into the Inn and, on some pretext, send out two of them first. That worked just fine for the first two; however, when Blue One came out with the other three, one of them, a *Wehrmacht* Colonel, decided to pull rank and insisted upon sitting in the heated cab. That was definitely not in the plan. Realizing this was an argument he couldn't win, Blue One pulled out his pistol. The other two officers, who had been heading for the back of the truck, turned to watch Blue One's reaction and, seeing him with the pistol, reached for their own. I grabbed for my pistol, yelling, "Blue One, shoot!"

As I got one of them, an MP38 opened up beside me and both men fell to the ground. Without turning to see who had shot, I jumped out to see if Blue One needed any help. He didn't. The Colonel lay on the ground as Blue One put a final shot through his head. He said quietly, "Let's get out of here," and jumped into the cab. I turned to see Martinson and Blue Ten making sure the other two were dead. We all jumped into the truck and the driver gunned it.

We didn't stop for the next 30 minutes, until we were clear of the town and on a back road in the middle of the woods to the West. Blue One and Blue Three came around and got in back with us. He didn't appear overly worried. "I don't think anyone saw the truck," he said. "At that time of night, by the time the police arrive, all they'll have is a story of one German officer sitting down with five others at a table in the restaurant. Two left and, a few minutes later, the other four left. There was some shooting, with three bodies and three missing officers.

"Sooner or later, some German soldiers – drivers and aides staying at the inn for the weekend, while their commanders had some business – will identify the three bodies and two of the missing officers. Nobody will know who the sixth officer was. There will be much confusion and conjecture, but I doubt anyone will connect the officers to a certain Castle a few miles West of the town for days."

"Why not?" someone asked.

"Given the secrecy surrounding the entire project at *Schloss Hülchrath*, it is extremely unlikely that any of the *Werwolfs'* aides or drivers knew anything about it or, for that matter, the destination of their Commanders' weekend business trip. By the time the *Werwolfs'* various Commanders are informed of their deaths, assuming any of them can put the pieces together, we should be long gone. It is my opinion that we should continue as planned; however, that is up to Blue Eight, according to my instructions."

I started to look around when I realized *I* was Blue eight. Mac was being clever again. The team didn't really need a leader unless something went wrong. Depending upon *what* went wrong, Blue One would normally be viewed as the decision-maker, being the man on the spot. Apparently, Mac trusted me more to make – or not make - an abort decision.

There comes a time in every operation when the wheels are turning, the die is cast, the cards are dealt, if you please, and you've got to carry on as planned and hope for the best. I can name you names, too many of them, of men I've known - and women, too - who died because some last-minute piece of information made them try to pull a switcheroo after the ball had been snapped and the backfield was in motion. When that point comes, to scramble the similes even further, you just take the phone off the hook and walk away from it. You don't want to hear what the guy at the other end of the line has to say. You've done your best, you've learned everything possible in the time at your disposal, and you don't want any more dope on any part of the situation, because it's too late and you can't do anything about it, anyway.

"I agree with Blue One. This will be our only chance at these *Werwolfs*. Let's do it."

We dragged the bodies out into the woods, got back in the truck and headed for the Castle.

Chapter 32

As we pulled up beside the checkpoint at *Schloss Hülchrath*, at a little after 1:30 in the morning, it appeared that our games with the insignia and papers were wasted effort, which was a good thing, considering we were short three sets. The guard who came out of the shed obviously was expecting us and recognized Blue One. He didn't even look in the back, just saluted and waved us on.

We pulled into the wide circular driveway leading to the entrance to the castle, and parked among a dozen or so other cars and trucks in a parking area opening off the driveway to the left side of the entrance. We all got out and stood there for a few moments, getting our bearings. I saw the two guest houses to the left of the parking area, with several trees in front of them. I looked at Martinson, who nodded at me. The trees would give us a hiding place so the soldiers wouldn't see us until we let them, once they were well out of the houses. I picked out a tree in front of the Commandant's house and pointed to it, telling Martinson and Blue Eleven, "I'll be there." They did likewise with two trees in front of the soldiers' house.

Seeing we were ready, Blue One said, "OK, let's go." The plan was for all 11 of us to go into the castle first and then Blue Eleven, Martinson and I would take our places outside once the inside soldier or soldiers were handled. As we opened the door, we saw two soldiers sitting at a small table playing cards. Apparently Commandant Weiss liked keeping his guards in pairs. They stood up and saluted as we entered. Blue One greeted them and asked if they could show us to our rooms. They seemed to like that idea. We were a little later than expected and they were losing sleep. As they turned toward the corridor leading to the bedrooms, Blue One grabbed one from behind, his hand covering the soldier's mouth, and expertly slit his throat. Martinson got the other one from behind with a garrote while Blue Three slipped a knife up under his ribcage into the heart....

After a pause to let the adrenaline rush subside, Blue One looked around at us. "Three minutes from right ... now" – we all checked our watches – "Silver Bullet starts in earnest. Move!"

As the others started down the corridor, Blue Eleven, Martinson and I went out the front door to take our positions. That left us over two minutes to wait for the shooting to begin....

My guys were alert. The almost simultaneous blasts of eight grenades going off at once was deafening, even through the walls of the castle, followed shortly thereafter by machine gun fire from eight weapons. In less than 10 seconds after the grenades went off, the two soldiers came flying out of the door, holding pistols in their hands. One was coming straight toward my location while, unfortunately, the other veered off at an angle, making it impossible to get them both at once. Taking the easy shot, I put half a magazine from the MP38 into the guy running toward me and then turned to get his partner. I saw him duck behind a tree a few feet from the one I had used, so I got back behind mine so I could see both his tree and the door to the guest house, figuring I'd take whomever showed up first.

About then, I heard machine-gun fire from the next yard. Considering the soldiers in the smaller guesthouse had most likely been asleep, they had pretty quick reflexes. That was the last coherent thought I had before the grenade went off. I briefly saw pieces of the soldier behind the tree fly out before the blast hit me....

I remembered Martinson assuring me that he had got the Commandant and, later, someone saying that the operation was a complete success - other than me, of course, our only casualty. I don't remember much else of that three-day trip other than pain.

Chapter 33

After a few more weeks of pain in a London hospital, I was transferred to a Washington hospital for a little plastic surgery and, thanks to Mac, a decision…

I once knew a singer, a terrific baritone with Metropolitan ambitions, whose voice left him suddenly for no apparent reason. And there was a sports car driver I remembered, headed for the big time, who cracked up badly and, although his injuries seemed to heal all right, never quite managed to win another race. Something had gone and he could never get it back. Sometimes, in a dangerous business, meeting the right kind of girl does it; suddenly you feel you've just got to keep on living for her, and you can't face the big risks any longer. Other times, you just come so close to death and survive that you're no longer willing to come that close again.

In our business specifically, sometimes there's a conscience factor. Although Mac had done his best to kill it, I still had a few remnants left. It had started with Frieda and continued with the necessary – but sick-making – butchery of the *Werwolfs*. Not the ones in the castle or the soldiers in front of the guest houses – they were fair game so far as I was concerned – or even the three in front of the *Wegberg Gasthaus*. My conscience, small as it was, wasn't bothered by that kind of killing or shooting a designated target at 300 yards, or even three feet. No, what bothered me a little was the cold-blooded murder of the seven unsuspecting *Werwolfs* who had eagerly jumped into the back of a truck with nothing on their minds but a weekend of good food and comradeship. Of course, what they would have been planning would have been bad for our side … but good from their viewpoint.

Who was I trying to kid? So it bothered me – I could live with it. Hell, I could even justify it. Over three years working for Mac had had a profound effect on my way of thinking, not that I had that far to go. We have a recognized oversupply of human beings; we can spare a few of the less desirable specimens. That might make me a monster with a rather dangerous philosophy, but there's a need in this world for monsters of the highly specialized, self-disciplined, narrowly focused kind, bound by a set of rules. OK, so the rules weren't the kind you'd expect, but rules they were, rigidly followed by Mac and his *M-Group*. Actually, I was quite proud of my membership.

So, what was the problem? Was I bothered by coming so close to dying? Well, yes; I'm rather fond of life, but not inordinately so. Not so much that I could no longer take the risks that went with the job. At least, I didn't think so – you never really know until the next time you have to.

I put down my empty iced tea glass, got up out of the chair with some minor effort, got in bed and turned out the light. Sleep was nowhere in sight, so I just lay there thinking. For some reason, I remembered dove hunting with my father in New Mexico, where we'd moved earlier from Minnesota. The dove's the greatest little game bird on this continent. I don't talk about it much nowadays - when you mention shooting perfectly legal game in season people act like you'd cut your mother's throat with a dull knife.

We'd had a dog with us, a big German Shorthaired Pointer named Buck. Old Buck had been imported straight from Europe by a wealthy rancher, a friend of Dad's, who'd then had a heart attack. He'd given Buck to Dad so a good dog wouldn't be, well, wasted on somebody who couldn't hunt him right. You don't use a pointing dog to find doves, of course, not like when you're hunting pheasants or quail. With doves, you just scout around until you find a place they're using, a field or spring or gravel pit, and you hide in the bushes and take them as they fly by. We worked Buck as a retriever on doves, to locate and bring in the birds that fell. They're hard little devils to find in any kind of cover without a dog, and Dad was very particular about shooting game and letting it go to waste. That evening, I remember, we were late getting home because we'd spent half an hour stomping through some tall weeds locating my last bird. Buck had been retrieving for Dad and hadn't seen it drop, but he finally found it. If we hadn't, we'd still be out there looking for that dove, I guess. Dad wasn't about to have a good day ruined by a lost bird.

I remember getting out of the old pickup in front of the house, letting Buck jump out of the rear on command, and gathering up the guns and hunting vests and shooting stools. It was a long reach for me into the pickup since I hadn't got my height yet. Dad had gone ahead to open the gate. He was waiting while I got a good grip on all my gear so I could follow.

He had said, "That was a fine shoot, Matthew, but we must rest that field tomorrow or we will burn it out; the doves will become frightened and stop using it." He didn't have a Scandinavian accent as much as a Scandinavian way of speaking. He went on, "Now you go feed the dog while I start plucking the birds."

I had a sharp picture in my mind of him standing there in his beat up Stetson and worn ranch clothes with the old Model 12 Winchester that had a slip-on rubber recoil pad to lengthen the stock to fit him, since he was a tall, long-armed man. He'd never, that I remembered, got around to having a longer stock made although he was always talking about it. I could see the little swinging gate and the rural-type mailbox on a post. The lettering on the box was easy to read: "Rt. 4, Box 75, Karl M. Helm."

Helm. Matthew L. Helm, son of Karl and Erika Helm. I guess I was thirteen or fourteen at the time. I was a feisty young fellow.

My mother always claimed we were distantly related to some old Scottish royalty. Although I'm Scandinavian, whose family is strictly anything? Quite a few Scots migrated to Sweden at one time or another. There was a guy named Glenmore. He had a claymore for hire and times were tough at home, so he went over a few hundred years back to swing his blade for a royal personage named Gustavus Adolphus, who happened to have employment for gents handy with edged weapons. Apparently he married and stayed on after the wars were over. My mother had documentation, charts, family trees and more in a pile of stuff I was paying storage charges on.   It seems that Robert Glenmore, Earl of Dalbright, if that's the proper way to say it, had two sons, Robert and Edward, in that order. Robert stayed in Scotland as far as I know. Being the oldest, I guess he had something to inherit if he stayed. Edward went to Sweden by way of Germany some time around 1631. He married over there and had kids, who married and had kids, and so forth, until my mother came along. She married, went to the U.S., and had me.

My father's side of the family apparently originated in Sweden, at least as far back as he had bothered to track, which was to the late 1500s and a Baron named Stjernhjelm. As Swedish titles go to all the children, I could have been a Baron, myself, but my folks renounced all foreign titles when they became American citizens. It's required, I understand, but it seems a shame.

In the midst of this half-dozing free-association, I suddenly sat straight up in bed. All at once, I had no more doubts. I knew what I was going to tell Mac. I was getting out of the assassin business. Not for any of the usual reasons – or perhaps for a little bit of *all* the usual reasons. Couple all the things I had been through in the last three years with my sense of family, passed on to me by my mother and father, and add in Beth…

No, not Beth – we hadn't known each other long enough for her specifically to be a reason – but the idea of a Beth. If I went back to work for Mac, I might never have a chance for a family of my own; hell, if I went back to Mac, I might be dead in a few weeks or months. I've long since faced the fact that, in the business I'd chosen for myself, I would probably die a little earlier than I otherwise might. Up until now, it had seemed a fair trade-off.

Now, I was having strange thoughts – thoughts of a family with a son or two, thoughts of a wife waiting at home when I got back from my nice, normal job where the greatest danger was the daily commute.

And it *could* be Beth. I hoped it *would* be Beth. But even if it wasn't, I *wanted* a Beth….

Chapter 34

The last time I saw Mac, he was sitting behind a desk in a shabby little office just off 12th Street in Washington. Somehow he always managed to arrange his offices, wherever they might be (I could remember one in London with a grim view of bombed-out buildings) so that he had a window behind him, making it hard to read his expression against the light, which I suppose was the idea.

"Here's your war record," he said as I came up to the desk. He shoved some papers towards me. "Study it carefully. Here are some additional notes on people and places you're supposed to have known. Memorize and destroy. And here are the ribbons you're entitled to wear, should you ever be called back into uniform."

I looked at them and grinned. "What, no Purple Heart?" I'd just spent three months in various hospitals. The official story was that a jeep had turned over on me while out on an assignment near Paris for Army Public Relations. Well, I suppose that scars from a Nazi grenade don't look a whole lot different than those from a demolished American jeep, especially when the more obvious bullet holes have been carefully erased by a discreet plastic surgeon.

He didn't smile. "Don't take these discharge papers too seriously, Eric. You're out of the Army, to be sure, but don't let it go to your head."

"Meaning what, sir?"

"Meaning that there are going to be a lot of chaps" - like all of us, he'd picked up some British turns of speech overseas - "impressing a lot of susceptible maidens with what brave, misunderstood fellows they were throughout the war, prevented by security from disclosing their heroic exploits to the world. There are also going to be a lot of hair-raising, revealing, and probably quite lucrative memoirs written." Mac looked up at me, as I stood before him. I had trouble seeing his face clearly, with that bright window behind him, but I could see his eyes. They were gray and cold. "I'm telling you this because your peacetime record shows certain literary tendencies. There'll be no such memoirs from this outfit. What we were, never was. What we did, never happened. Keep that in mind, Captain Helm." His use of my military title and real name marked the end of a part of my life. I was outside now.

I said, "I had no intention of writing anything of the kind, sir."

"Perhaps not. But you're to be married soon, I understand, to an attractive young lady you met at a local hospital. Congratulations. But remember what you were taught, Captain Helm. You do not confide in anyone, no matter how close to you. You do not even hint, if the question of wartime service is raised, that there are tales you could tell if you were only at liberty to do so. No matter what the stakes, Captain Helm, no matter what the cost to your pride or reputation or family life, no matter how trustworthy the person involved, you reveal nothing, not even that there's something to reveal." He gestured towards the papers on the desk. "Your cover isn't perfect, of course. No cover is. You may be caught in an inconsistency. You may even meet someone with whom you're supposed to have been closely associated during some part of the war, who, never having heard of you, calls you a liar and perhaps worse. We've done all we can to protect you against such a contingency, for our sakes as well as yours, but there's always the chance of a slip. If it happens, you'll stick to your story, no matter how awkward the situation becomes. You'll lie calmly and keep on lying. To everyone, even your wife. Don't tell her that you could explain everything if only you were free to speak. Don't ask her to trust you because things aren't what they seem. Just look her straight in the eye and lie."

"I understand," I said. "May I ask a question?"

"Yes."

"No disrespect intended, sir, but how are you going to enforce all that, now?"

I thought I saw him smile faintly, but that wasn't likely. He wasn't a smiling man. He said, "You've been discharged from the Army, Captain Helm. You've not been discharged from us. How can we give you a discharge, when we don't exist?"

And that was all of it, except that as I started for the door with my papers under my arm he called me back.

I turned snappily. "Yes, Sir."

"You're a good man, Eric. One of my best. Good luck."

It was something, from Mac, and it pleased me, but as I went out and, from old habit, walked a couple of blocks away from the place, before taking a cab to where Beth was waiting. I knew that he need have no fear of my confiding in her against orders. I'd have told her the truth if it had been allowed, of course, to be honest with her; but my bride-to-be was a gentle and sensitive New England girl, and I wasn't unhappy to be relieved, by authority, of the necessity of telling her I'd been a good man in that line of business. It was time to put that business behind me once and for all. And what better way than with a sweet and soft and innocent girl who had never seen a dead man, except perhaps in an antiseptic hospital bed.

When the cab stopped, I reached into my pocket for some money. My fingers felt the knife and, for some reason, I pulled it out. What I had was a folding hunting knife of German Solingen steel. There were two blades, a corkscrew, and no tricks except that when the large blade was opened it locked into place, so it couldn't close accidentally on your fingers, no matter what resistance it met in dressing out game - or in any other occupation you might find for it. I remembered taking it off the body of the Nazi general after my own knife had jammed and broken between his ribs and Tina has finished the job with the butt of a rifle. It wasn't as big as a fighting knife ought to be, by a long shot, and it wasn't worth a damn for throwing, being balanced all wrong. But it was inconspicuous enough so that I could carry it anywhere, and even be seen paring my fingernails with it, without attracting much attention except for my bad manners. I'd carried it through the last year of the war, never having occasion to use it, as the saying goes, in anger.

As I paid the cab driver, I considered giving him the knife as a tip. I grimaced at the thought of such an empty gesture and put it back in my pocket. Memories and all, the knife was mine, and I would keep it.

Never mind a girl named Tina, with the violet eyes and deadly skills, who not only had seen several dead men, but had made many of them that way. Tina, who might be waiting somewhere over there, waiting for someone who no longer existed. I turned and started up the stairs to where Beth waited…

The End

Made in the USA
San Bernardino, CA
25 September 2014